CHA

The

me of her

gs it off. At the same
time, she spins                          and mystery."
                                              —*Houston Post*

"Impish play on words and a generous dash of wit lend
MacLeod mysteries their trademark—sheer fun. Her fans grow
with every book she writes, and deservedly so."
                              —*Alfred Hitchcock's Mystery Magazine*

ALSO BY CHARLOTT

*Published by*

SARAH KELLING & M

PROFESSOR PET

# CHARLOTTE MacLEOD

# The Convivial Codfish

**A SARAH KELLING &
MAX BITTERSOHN MYSTERY**

**new york
www. ibooks. net**

DISTRIBUTED BY SIMON & SCHUSTER, INC.

A Publication of ibooks, inc.

An ibooks, inc. Book

Distributed by Simon & Schuster, Inc.
1230 Avenue of the Americas, New York, NY 10020

ibooks, inc.
24 West 25th Street
New York, NY 10010

The ibooks World Wide Web Site Address is:
http://www.ibooks.net

ISBN 0-7434-7493-7
First ibooks, inc. printing August 2003
10 9 8 7 6 5 4 3 2 1

Cover design by j. vita

Printed in the U.S.A.

*For Claudia Kren*

CHARLOTTE MacLEOD

# **The Convivial Codfish**

# CHAPTER 1

Exalted Chowderhead Jeremy Kelling, of the Beacon Hill Kellings, gazed benignly around the luncheon table at his eighteen Comrades of the Convivial Codfish. Wineglass raised, he proposed the Ancient and Time-Honoured Toast:

'Here's to us!'

'And to hell with the rest of 'em,' roared the Comrades in one great voice.

'Down the hatch, Comrades!'

'Bottoms up,' shouted seventeen of them.

'A dead whale or a stove boat,' yelped Comrade Wouter Tolbathy. Nobody paid any attention. They were used to Wouter.

The glasses were drained. The Exalted Chowderhead dabbed at his lips with a black-bordered napkin to which a spray of holly had been affixed, minus its berries and upside-down.

'I hereby declare our annual Scrooge Day to be in session. 'Tis the season to be snarly. Whither art thou, Marley's Ghost?'

'Present and clanking, Exalted.' Hung with safe deposit boxes, piggy banks, petty cash vouchers, a streetcar conductor's nickel-plated coin sorter, and fragments of an old cash register, Formerly Exalted Comrade Tom Tolbathy rattled smartly to attention.

'Canst thou produce the Detected Object?'

'I canst, Exalted. At least I think I canst.'

Considerably impeded by his plethora of piggy banks, Marley's Ghost reached under the table and tugged forth the chosen artifact.

'God, is there no bottom limit to the depravity of human imagination?' murmured Comrade Billingsgate.

Last year's affront to his aesthetic sensibilities had been a Stryofoam elf with sequined eyeballs that lit up and twinkled. This year, it was an inflatable plastic Rudolph the Red-Nosed Reindeer standing four feet high from hooves to antlers, wearing a red-and- green chicken feather tutu. Even the Exalted Chowderhead winced, but went manfully on with the ceremony.

'Ghost of Christmas Past, what sayest thou?'

Comrade Dowl lumbered to his feet. 'Bah, humbug,' he growled.

'Bah, humbug!' the Comrades howled back.

'Ghost of Christmas Present, may we have your report?'

Comrade Ogham settled his wreath of wilted mistletoe more dashingly over his left ear, gave the assemblage a good look at his teeth clear back to the bicuspids, and replied sweetly, 'Bah, humbug. Comrades, I hope you've followed your Exalted Chowderhead's sterling example and been bad little boys this year.'

'Bah, humbug!' they replied, all but Jeremy Kelling  He maintained a dignified silence until the dust had quit falling from the finely moulded old plaster ceiling.

'Ghost of Christmas to Come, pray speak '

Formerly Grand Exalted Chowderhead E. Wripp groped for the edge of the table  Thus supported, he managed to hoist himself halfway out of his chair. 'Bah, humbug,' he quavered

This was Obed Ogham's idea of fun, Jeremy Kelling thought sourly  He'd been the one to insist on Wripp for the role  Dash it, the Comrades didn't need to be reminded what sort of shape they themselves might be in a few Christmases hence  Nor was it even decent, let alone amusing, to use poor old Wripp as a pawn in a tasteless joke

Jeremy Kelling himself was a relative infant among the Comrades of the Convivial Codfish, being still on the sunny side of seventy  He'd had to wait until the belated demise of his own Great-Uncle Serapis, the only other *bon vivant* in the

Kelling clan, before he could even be considered for membership, which was strictly limited and generally went by inheritance Then he'd had to work his way up through the ranks. For years he'd been dreaming of the time when he, little Jem, would get to wear the Great Chain with its perch-sized sterling silver codfish pendant and sit at the head of the table. Only this past November, when the Comrades gave formal thanks to be rid of their previous Exalted Chowderhead and announced themselves ready to take on an evil they wotted not yet of, had he been raised to august rank This was his first whack at chairing a meeting and if that bastard Ogham thought he could crab Jem's act, he could think again, by gad. Avoiding the Ghost of Christmas Present's no doubt sardonic leer, Jem swept a gallant bow in the oldest member's direction

'Thank you, Formerly Grand Exalted, and a hearty bah, humbug to you. Comrades, a triple rejoinder for the Ghost of Christmas Yet to Come '

They gave it with a will. Perhaps some felt this might be the last bah, humbug their once-puissant leader would ever receive. It was a poignant moment. Even Obed Ogham seemed to feel some small pricking of remorse for his ill-judged prank. At any rate, he appeared to humbug with due reverence and sobriety

But sobriety was not the object of this gathering, and Jeremy Kelling would have been the last Scrooge to pretend it was. 'Bob Cratchit,' he ordered, 'get to work or I'll fine you thruppence and take away your coal hod.'

'Aye, verily, Exalted.' Bob Cratchit, known to his underlings as Mr Ashbroom, to his wife as Edward, and to a lady in an apartment on Joy Street as Cuddles, cringed around the table refilling the wineglasses in a properly servile manner.

'And now, Tiny Tim, may we have the malediction?'

Comrade Durward, who had taken off his spectacles so that he wouldn't be able to see the Detested Object, put them on again and peered around the table in search of his wineglass. He located it at last two points southeast of his plate and succeeded after a few tries in making safe hand contact with the stem. At last he rose to speak his one immortal line.

'Bah, humbug, every one.'

Bob Cratchit sniffled. 'Fair tugs at the 'eart strings, don't 'e?'

'Bah, humbug, you old humbug,' snarled Obed Ogham. 'As for you, brat, one more word out of you and I'll splinter your crutch. Comrades, do you suppose Scrooge is ever going to give us anything to eat?'

Not by word, glance, or so much as a flaring nostril did Jeremy Kelling indicate that he found the plastic reindeer only the second most detested object present. He merely got on with the agenda.

'Marley's Ghost, prithee conjure up a Suitable Receptacle.'

'Forthwith, Exalted.'

Tom Tolbathy, at least, could be relied on not to pad his part. Managing his chains as deftly as his grandmother had done her bustle, he clanked away to the corner of the meeting room and returned with a tinsel-bedecked garbage can. Jeremy Kelling gave him a nod of thanks, then raised the Detested Object high above his head.

'Comrades of the Convivial Codfish, let us keep Christmas in our own fashion.'

'Thar she blows,' said Wouter Tolbathy. It was a surprisingly relevant remark, for Woulter.

Rudolph the Red-Nosed Reindeer proved too big for the Suitable Receptacle. Marley's Ghost solved the dilemma by whipping a jackknife out from among his impedimenta and sticking Rudolph in the rump, to tumultuous applause. The Exalted Chowderhead them crammed the deflated wad of repulsion into the garbage can, flung the feathered tutu in after it, and dusted his hands.

'Whoop, whoop, halloo. I am as merry as a schoolboy. Cratchit, the bottle. Mrs Cratchit, the chowder.'

It would have been unthinkable for the Comrades of the Convivial Codfish to order anything but genuine Boston fish chowder, made without any superfluous abominations, and that was what they got. The waitress who brought it, however, albeit an acceptable Mrs Cratchit in every other respect, had been so misguided as to adorn her bodice with a superfluous abomination in the shape of a whimsical Christmas corsage. Comrade Dork voiced the general outrage

'Exalted Chowderhead, I move Mrs Cratchit be requested to park that bedizenment in the Suitable Receptacle, as constituting an affront to the curmudgeonly spirit of Scrooge Day and to the disgruntlement for which we so proudly stand '

'Second the motion,' growled the Ghost of Christmas Past.

'Any objections or abstentions?' asked Jeremy Kelling

Comrade Durward raised his hand 'I can't see what the fuss is all about.'

'Can you see Mrs Cratchit?'

'Er—actually, no.' He took off his spectacles, wiped the enormously thick lenses with his napkin, put them on again, and peered earnestly into the face next to him. 'Oh, hello, Wouter. I thought you were Tom.'

'I am,' said Marley's Ghost 'Wouter's over there.'

'Oh.' Comrade Durward took off his spectacles again, and subsided. Jeremy Kelling ruled him out of order and appointed himself to unpin it, feigning not to hear the lewd asides from Obed Ogham

Mollified by his assurance that she'd be allowed to retrieve her corsage afterward, Mrs Cratchit served the chowder. Excellent chowder it was, and lustily did the Comrades bale it in Even their Exalted Chowderhead forgot the cares of office and concentrated on getting his full share while maintaining a properly Scrooge-like demeanor. It wasn't until he had laid down his spoon and untied his black-bordered napkin from beneath his nethermost jowl that Jem Kelling noticed a horrible vacancy over his waistcoat. He was no longer wearing the Great Chain

'The Codfish,' he gasped 'It's gone!'

'It fell into the Receptacle, you jackass,' retorted Comrade Twitchett, who had not spoken at all until now, except for an occasional humbug

'I didn't hear it clink '

'Naturally not  You're deaf as a haddock and drunk as a skunk '

This intellectual repartee was right up the Comrades' alley  They varied and embellished the theme while Jem bellowed for Marley's Ghost to go get the goddamn Receptacle and bring it back. That done, he personally removed the corsage, the deflated Rudolph, and the feather tutu, shook them out to no avail, and at last stuck his head inside the Receptacle, to the accompaniment of coarse ribaldries

'The Codfish isn't there,' he groaned

'Then it's under the table where you usually wind up, you old souse,' replied the Ghost of Christmas Present

It was not  It wasn't anywhere  Those cumbrous silver links, that piscatorial pendant that had so short a time ago rested in splendour atop Jeremy Kelling's neat little paunch had vanished like the chowders of yesteryear.

'You've taken it off and forgotten to put it back on,' said Bob Cratchit, forgetting to cringe. 'Softening of the brain, that's all. Nothing to worry about. I'll serve the port, shall I?'

All hailed the suggestion except the Exalted Chowderhead  While the decanter went around and the Comrades waxed, despite their worst intentions, merry; Jeremy Kelling brooded  Where in hell had the damn thing got to? It couldn't have fallen off. Those massive, overlapping links had been clinched together for aeons to come by an old-time artisan who'd known whereof he clinched. There was no

clasp to come unfastened  The only way to remove the chain
would have been to lift it over his head

And that had not happened. So experienced a toper as J.
Lemuel Alexander Kelling Kelling could hardly have got
drunk enough on a paltry four glasses of Chardonnay
Sauvignon not to notice a trick like that. Furthermore, where
could it have got to? A damn great thing that weighed about
five pounds and had six inches of codfish attached to it was
no mere bauble you could stuff out of sight in your hip
pocket  None of the Comrades had been out of his sight since
he'd donned the Great Chain, except when one of them had
required to be excused for nonceremonial reasons. He himself hadn't left the room once. They didn't call him Old
Ironpants for nothing, by gad!

As Bob Cratchit continued his appointed rounds, speculation about the Great Chain's disappearance grew more
imaginative  Everybody accused everybody else of codnap-
ping  Comrades took to visiting the men's room in squads, to
make sure nobody was trying to sneak the Codfish off in his
codpiece.

Mrs Cratchit was exonerated, firstly because it would
have been ungallant to accuse her, secondly because she was
found on inquiry to be somebody's mother, and thirdly
because she'd had her hands full ever since she'd entered the
room; initially with the chowder tureen and and latterly with
Obed Ogham. She was allowed to gather her corsage and
depart in peace.

At last a thorough search of the room was conducted, with
all the Comrades crawling around the floor on hands and
knees making what they fancied to be reindeer noises; except
for Wouter Tolbathy, who chose to be a wyvern and probably was. Most of them appeared to regard the Great Chain's
disappearance as a jolly jape, and to be confident it would
turn up at the next meeting in some arcane guise.

Jeremy Kelling was not so sanguine. His first act on

returning to his Beacon Hill apartment was to fight off the ministrations of his faithful henchman Egburt, who took it for granted Mr Jem must be sick because he'd come home from the luncheon sober and perturbed instead of sloshed and jolly  His second was to put in an emergency call to his recently acquired nephew-in-law, Max Bittersohn

## CHAPTER 2

'Max,' howled Jem, 'I've lost the Codfish.'

Even though he'd taken a long leap away from his own family tree, Max retained many of its traditional values  Among the Bittersohns, grown men didn't go around losing codfish  Grown men worked, albeit they were entitled to be merry in their labour  Grown men improved their minds with serious study and their souls with deeds of noble self-sacrifice  Grown men looked after their wives and their kids, if they had any which Max didn't as yet, and had certain responsibilities to the *ganze mishpoche*, even when their family connections had grown to include uncles-in-law like Jeremy Kelling

Though he still hadn't figured out why some of his new wife's relatives were allowed to run loose, Max remembered his duty and delivered what he thought might possibly be a suitable reply

'I knew a man who lost a stuffed muskellunge once.'

He'd flubbed it again. Jem was irate.

'Dash it, man, cease your persiflage. The Great Chain of the Comrades of the Convivial Codfish is a sacred relic. Like the grasshopper on the Faneuil Hall weathervane, or George Washington's teeth,' he added to emphasize the gravity of the situation  'It disappeared some time after I'd put the Detested Object into the Suitable Receptacle.'

'That would be as reasonable a time as any, no doubt,'

Max answered. 'You don't suppose it fell into the receptacle?'

'How the hell could it? The blasted chain was around my neck There was no way it could have got there unless I fell in, too. Which I can assure you I did not. Damn it, I'm not drunk Egbert can testify to that.'

Now it was getting ridiculous. 'Put him on,' said Max.

Egbert, to their mutual amazement, was able to vouch for his employer's unprecedented sobriety. 'It's very worrisome, Mr Max. I've never seen him this way before. Except sometimes on the morning after,' he qualified, for Egbert was a truthful man when circumstances did not require him to be otherwise. 'I think he might accurately be described as shaken to the core '

'Good God! He can't be that bad.'

'Who can't?' Max's wife, Sarah, had just come into the room

'Your Uncle Jem. Egbert says he's shaken to the core. Put Jem back on, Egbert. Come here, *angela mia*.'

By holding the receiver a little way out from his ear and Sarah as close as possible to his chest, Max was able to include her in the conversation. There'd been too damned many years when he had no Sarah to hold and he was not about to miss an opportunity. Theoretically, of course, he now had every chance in the world. In fact, his crazy profession kept him away from her far too often.

Despite the necessary sacrifices, though, Max loved his work as a tracker-down of vanished valuables. The disappearance of any sacred relic, even a codfish, acted on him as a mayfly on a trout; and any codfish that could reduce Jeremy Kelling to a state of palpitating sobriety gave him a glorious excuse to satisfy his sense of family duty and indulge his second-favourite occupation at one swoop.

Sarah was interested, too. By calling on Max's expertise and forcing her uncle to talk sense for once in his life, she managed to obtain for her husband a complete and perhaps

even reasonably accurate account of the bizarre occurrence.
Jem was all set to tell it again, but Max wasn't about to listen.

'Okay, Jem, you've told me that. How much is the chain
worth?'

'Worth? What do you mean worth? It's priceless, damn it.
As a historic relic—'

'Relic of a thousand binges,' snapped his niece. 'Quit,
sputtering and tell Max what it's made of'

'Solid silver, of course.'

Goaded by Sarah, Jem managed a description of sorts 'I
can show you photographs, if they'd help,' he finished after
he'd dragged them floundering through a sea of in-
coherencies and profane interjections

'Why the hell didn't you say so?' growled Max, rubbing
his hand up and down Sarah's spine and thinking of all the
things he'd rather be doing than standing here listening to an
old rip blether on about a missing codfish 'Okay, Jem. I'll
drop over sometime soon and take a look'

'How soon? Dash it, Max, this is urgent business'

'Could we pinpoint the urgent? What's your next meeting?
April Fools' Day?'

'Curse you,' roared Jem, 'is nothing sacred to your disgusting generation? We meet on Valentine's Day, February
fourteenth I have to skewer a pink satin heart on the end of a
cavalry sabre at full gallop and deposit it in the Suitable
Receptacle And for your information, whippersnapper, the
Comrades do not celebrate the date to which you sneeringly
alluded Our April meeting's on the twenty-seventh, Ulysses
S Grant's birthday'

'I'm not surprised,' Sarah answered 'Do simmer down,
Uncle Jem Max will think of something He always does'

'Guess what I'm thinking right now,' Max murmured into
her soft hair

'Sorry to disappoint you, darling,' she told him, 'but
Cousin Brooks will be here in about two minutes to put up
the curtain rods.'

Max had forgotten about the curtain rods. Understandably, perhaps. He hated all those fiddling-around-the-house jobs Sarah's first husband had been so good at. Alexander would have had them up by now. Damn it, was he never going to quit being jealous of a dead man?

'Why didn't you remind me?' he growled. 'I told you I'd do them '

'So you did, last week and the week before. Cousin Brooks is going to do them this afternoon. That's the difference between you and him. One of the less important differences.'

She reached up to tug at his hair. Max had wonderful hair, thick and wavy and so dark a brown it might almost have been black. Sarah's own was just plain brown, though it did provide an agreeable frame for her squarish, rather pale, altogether delightful face. Her eyes were greenish hazel His were either blue or grey, she'd never been able to decide which. Among the multiramose Kelling clan, it was generally conceded that Sarah and her new husband didn't make a bad-looking couple.

Of course this Bittersohn fellow, whoever he might be, was far less handsome than the late Alexander Kelling; but so was everybody else. At least Max wasn't twenty-four years older than Sarah. He did make pots of money with that detective agency of his. And it was art, not divorces All things considered, almost everyone except Cousin Mabel was willing to concede Sarah might have done worse for herself.

They'd been married last June in the back yard at Ireson's Landing Sarah's cousin Dolph had given the bride away because he'd have raised hell if she hadn't let him. Max's nephew Mike had been best man for the same excellent reason Jed Lomax the caretaker and his crippled wife had been honoured guests. Cousin Theonia had baked the wedding cake; Max's sister Miriam had made the knishes Sarah's boarding-house confederates Mariposa and Charles had stage-managed the affair Nobody had got killed, or drunk beyond reasonable limits, or stung by a bee. Nobody had fought with anybody. Some people might have thought it dull, but Max and Sarah hadn't.

They'd been honeymooning ever since by fits and starts as Max's work allowed, camping out in the little apartment over the carriage house between trips until winter's advent drove them back to town.

At the old Kelling brownstone on Beacon Hill they'd had literally no place to lay their heads. Sarah'd done too good a job filling it with boarders and hadn't had the heart to put anyone out. Max was glad. It would have galled him to share her with a houseful of other people and her memories of her first marriage. He was far happier paying a preposterous monthly rent for a small apartment that had providentially fallen vacant in the house next door and dropping over for meals with Brooks, Theonia, and the paying guests once or twice a week.

They still weren't settled in. Sarah was running her legs off shopping for furniture and trying to cope for the first time with the double demands of Christmas and Chanukah, not to mention her own adjustments to a second set of in-laws. Max had a new client clamouring for a stolen Van Dyke, and much unfinished business on his hands. Neither of them had leisure to worry about Jeremy Kelling's silver codfish, and neither gave it more than a passing thought until Egbert turned up on their brand-new doormat the following evening.

Sarah let him in. 'Egbert, what a nice surprise. What's happened now?'

'It's Mr Jem, Mrs Sarah. He's fallen down the front hall stairway.'

Sarah stared at him. 'You don't mean the inside stairs? Egbert, he couldn't have  Uncle Jem loathes going over those stairs.'

'The elevator got stuck on the top floor, Mrs Sarah.'

That was possible, she knew. Jeremy and Egbert lived in a

block of flats that had been carved out of an old town house. There was an elevator dating from 1905 or thereabout, roughly the size of a phone booth. It wouldn't work unless both the inner and the outer door had been properly shut and latched by whoever had used it last.

When that happened, one either used the stairs or made a fuss. Jem's usual procedure was to send Egbert after the elevator, or else bellow up the shaft until some other tenant was goaded into going out and fixing the doors. In desperate situations, however, such as when Egbert wasn't around, nobody answered his calls, and he'd run out of gin, Jem had been known to stomp angrily down the one flight of stairs from his second-floor apartment. This, evidently, had been one of those times. Now Mr Jem was over at Phillips House with a brand-new stainless steel ball where the joint of his left femur used to be. Egbert thought Mrs Sarah and Mr Max would want to know.

'Yes, of course,' Sarah told him. 'Egbert, this is ghastly. Bad enough for Uncle Jem, of course, but think of those poor nurses who'll have to put up with him. Have you any idea how it happened? Did you get to talk to him?'

'I got to listen, Mrs Sarah. How it started was, he'd sent me out to do some Christmas shopping for him. Well, you know what the stores are like this time of year, so I was gone most of the afternoon. I got back to the house about five o'clock, dead beat, and what should I find when I opened the front door but Mr Jem sprawled on the vestibule floor, yelling his head off. As soon as I realized he wasn't able to stand up, I ran upstairs to call the ambulance and get him a tot of brandy. That dulled the pain and calmed him down enough so he could tell me what he was doing there. He said Fuzzleys' had phoned about a quarter to five and told him his whiskers were ready, but he'd have to hurry because they were closing in fifteen minutes. So he'd gone charging down the stairs like a damned old water buffalo. I beg your pardon, Mrs Sarah, but—'

'Don't apologize, Egbert. Naturally you're upset. Sit down and catch your breath. Max, Egbert's here. Bring him a drink, would you please? Uncle Jem's had an accident.'

Oh, Christ! What now? Max put down the newspaper with which he'd just got himself settled in one of their brand-new easy chairs and fetched the whisky. While Egbert sipped the restorative, Max shook his head in hopeless wonderment

'What was the big rush about the whiskers?'

'Don't ask me, Mr Max. There was no earthly need for him to go rushing off half-cocked. I could perfectly well have picked them up for him in the morning, but you know Mr Jem. He wanted those whiskers.'

'For the Tolbathys' railroad party, I suppose,' said Sarah. 'He told me he was going to dress up in Great-Uncle Nathan's Prince Albert and get some dundreary whiskers and impersonate Jay Gould.'

'Are you sure Jay Gould had dundrearies?'

'I haven't the faintest idea. That's how Uncle Jem visualized the role, anyway. He's been in a dither about this party for weeks.'

'Why a railroad party?' Max was still determined, somehow, to make sense of all this.

'Because the Tolbathys have their own train, I suppose.'

'The hell they do!'

'Oh yes,' Egbert corroborated. 'There's a locomotive, and a parlour car with red plush settees and gilded mirrors, and a dining car and a caboose.'

'That's nice. Any particular reason?'

'I think Tom inherited them,' said Sarah. 'His people were in railroads back when there were railroads to be into. They have this enormous estate somewhere out in the western wilds, with tracks laid through the woods, and they're planning a big Christmas bash on the train. They're going to tootle along with a string ensemble playing Victor Herbert waltzes and a fountain spouting champagne and I don't know what all. Everyone's supposed to gather at North Station in Gay Nineties costume and take the B&M out to Concord or Lincoln or somewhere From there they'll be driven to the Tolbathys' in an antique London bus.'

'My God! Jem will have apoplexy at missing a bash like that '

'He was in a highly aggravated state of profanity when I left him,' said Egbert 'They were going to give him a sedative.'

'They'd never shut him up without one.' Sarah poured Egbert another shot of whisky, for he was an old and beloved friend 'Here, drink this, then Max will walk you home You don't mind, do you, darling? I'd go, too, but I have a million cards still to write Oh dear, I do hope Uncle Jem will be out of the hospital for Christmas. Dolph and Mary will be sick if he doesn't show up for their big family get-together You know what a glorious time he and Dolph always have calling each other awful names. I'll go over to see him tomorrow morning You'd better get some extra rest. You're going to need it before this is over '

'Truer words were never spoken, Mrs Sarah By the way, Mr Max, he asked me to—er—remind you about the Codfish '

Max grinned 'In precisely those words?'

'Not precisely, Mr Max.'

'Well, tell him I'm hot on the trail. One for the road?'

'Thank you, but I'd better be getting back to the flat. Some of Mr Jem's lady friends may be calling.'

'No doubt. Let's hit the road, then.'

Max put on his coat and set out with Egbert over the Hill from Tulip Street to Pinckney. 'Who else is going on this train ride? The rest of the Codfish crowd?'

'Some of them, at any rate. I know Mr Wripp will be there. He was recently operated on for cataracts, and Mrs Tolbathy thought the outing would do him good. She's a very kind-hearted lady.'

'That's nice, What office does Wripp hold?'

'Mr Wripp is a Formerly Grand Exalted Chowderhead. Being now ninety-six years of age, he appears content to rest on past laurels. Oh, yes, and Mr Jem was saying Mr Ogham was also invited. So maybe it's just as well Mr Jem won't be able to go, after all.'

'Why? Don't Jem and this Ogham get along?'

'None of the Kelling family care much for Mr Ogham, Mr Max He's the one who sued Mr Percy Kelling for two dollars and forty-three cents he claimed he'd been overcharged This was after Mr Percy's accounting firm had managed to get back one and a half million dollars Mr Ogham's second vice-president had embezzled.'

'Oh, that's the one Dolph was telling me about it Ogham's one of the few things I've ever heard him and Jem agree on, come to think of it How come Jem's still in the same club with him?'

'There have always been Kellings and Oghams among the Comrades of the Convivial Codfish. Neither of them wants to cede his ancestral right to the other Noblesse oblige, you might say.'

Max supposed you might, though he couldn't think why. 'But don't the Tolbathys know Jem and Ogham are feuding?'

'It's only Mr Ogham who feuds, Mr Max Mr Jem maintains a haughty silence. Or so he says.'

The notion of Jem's maintaining a haughty silence under any circumstances was a hard one to swallow, but Max didn't say so He liked Egbert, and he could see Jem's accident had been a serious blow to that errant knight's long-suffering squire.

'Furthermore,' Egbert was going on, 'Mr Ogham's related to Mrs Tolbathy. Comrade Whet is, too, but he won't be there. He's in Nairobi on business. Mr Jem was intending to escort Mrs Whet.'

'Mrs Whet's a good-looking woman, well dressed, a bit on

the hefty side but not fat, right? Enjoys a good time, holds her liquor like a lady, and knows when to go home to Papa.'

'You know Mrs Whet, Mr Max?'

'No, but I know Jem. So the party's just a bunch of friends and relatives?'

'Pretty much, I believe. It won't be a large group. I don't suppose the train would accommodate more than thirty or forty in any kind of comfort It's not like a regular train, you know, and there's just the two cars They'll need the caboose for the catering and so forth, I should think.'

'Rather an elaborate bash to lay on for so small a crowd, isn't it?'

'Well, the biggest expense would be the train,' Egbert pointed out, 'and they've already got that.'

'True enough Here's the old homestead I'll come in with you '

'Thanks, Mr Max, but you mustn't feel obliged.'

'I'd like to, if you don't mind I want to see the place where Jem fell.'

'Just a moment, then. My key must be—ah, here we are. The staircase is just inside the door, as you see, and Mr Jem was right here at the foot, lying up against the newel post. He said he bounced against every single stair as he slid down That must be how he broke his hip '

Max took a look at the thick oaken stairway and the marble floor, and grunted 'Damn good thing he landed on his backside instead of his head. Who uses this stairway, as a rule?'

'Nobody, unless the elevator gets stuck. I used to, but I must say I don't relish that kind of exercise at my time of life, unless I'm forced into it.'

'Did Jem tell you how he happened to head for the stairs? Did he try the elevator first?'

'He told me the power went off just before he got the phone call from Fuzzleys'. He noticed because he'd been listening to the radio and thought it had suddenly gone on the blink, but then he realized that electric clock Mrs Appie gave him so he wouldn't always be late for appointments had stopped, too. That meant the elevator wouldn't be working, either, so he didn't even try pushing the button but just headed for the stairs. It was just tough luck, I suppose, him being in a hurry and not watching where he stepped. And being in such a dither about losing the Codfish.'

In the meagre overhead light, Egbert looked like an elderly beagle, grown grey around the muzzle, perplexed by the vicissitudes he no longer had any particular urge to cope with 'You know, Mr Max, my poor old mother always used to say bad luck came in threes Do you think we can count having to miss the Tolbathys' party as Mr Jem's third?'

'I'm not sure we ought to count any of this as bad luck,' Bittersohn answered 'What happened to the clothes Jem was wearing when he fell? Are they still at the hospital?'

'No, they're upstairs, as a matter of fact I thought I'd better bring them back with me so he wouldn't get any notions about trying to leave before the doctor says he can. It seemed silly to lug them all the way to Tulip Street and back, so I dropped them off here on my way to your place I thought I'd look them over before I went to bed It'll give me something to do.'

'Let's have a look at them together.'

The tiny elevator was sitting in the foyer, both its safety doors meticulously fastened Word of Jem's fall must have got around among the tenants Since neither of them was portly, Max and Egbert managed to fit themselves in at the same time and ride up to the second floor At the flat, Egbert showed Max where Jem's clothes lay, and Max, to his astonishment, took out a magnifying glass to examine the trousers It took only a moment to find what he was looking for.

'Aha! See that, Egbert?'

'A grease spot on the seat of his pants?' Egbert was horrified. 'Mr Max, you don't think I'd have let Mr Jem go out looking like that? I sponged and pressed those pants only this morning.'

Max nodded. 'Hand me the shoes, will you?'

There it was, a wide, dark, greasy smudge clear across the left sole. The sole of the right shoe was clean and dry. Egbert gasped. Max didn't even look surprised.

'That's it, Egbert  Got a flashlight?'

'Oh yes, right here  I always leave one in Mr Jem's nightstand, just in case.'

'Come on, then. I'm curious to see which stair got buttered.'

## CHAPTER 3

It was the third step from the landing, and it was Egbert who spotted the brownish glob under the tread

'Would this be what you're looking for, Mr Max?'

Bittersohn rubbed a little of the slippery paste between his thumb and finger, then sniffed. 'It sure as hell would  Bowling alley wax, I'd say offhand. Take a look at this varnish on the step. Wouldn't you say some kind of solvent has been used here recently? To clean off what was left of the wax, we can presume. Would that have been the janitor?'

Egbert snorted. 'Not unless he's got religion all of a sudden. He sweeps the hallway and stairs once a week, and that's it. Otherwise, he comes around the back way every morning about half past eight to pick up the trash we put out, and we don't see hide nor hair of him till the next day  My guess is that whoever smeared this wax on the stairs came back after we'd got Mr Jem out, and cleaned it off. Only he didn't do a thorough job because he was in a hurry. Or she was  Floor wax is the sort of trick a woman would think of, I dare say  But who'd do a thing like that to Mr Jem?'

'Good question,' said Max. 'What do you say we go call on the neighbours?'

The third floor was occupied by an elderly widow, her maid, and her cook. The widow was out playing bridge, with the maid in attendance. The cook was delighted to have company.

'Herself took Mary along because she doesn't like riding in taxis alone at night, so I'm all on my own,' she explained 'Could I give you a cup of tea in the kitchen, now? It's dull here by myself.'

Before Egbert could utter a scandalized refusal, Max was seated at the table. 'This is really kind of you, ma'am. I see your electric clock's right on the dot,' he added in a by-the-way tone, checking his own wristwatch against it.

'Has to be,' the cook told him. 'Herself expects her meals served prompt to the second '

'Haven't had to reset it lately, have you?'

'Why would I do that, now? I never touch that clock, except maybe to give it a wipe with the duster when the spirit moves me.'

Cook knew who the two men were, or assumed she did, and was more than ready to chat about whatever they wanted to hear. It soon became clear, though, that she hadn't much to tell. The couple on the fourth floor had gone off to Palm Beach with the rest of the bigwigs and weren't expected back until after Easter. She personally hadn't known a thing about poor Mr Kelling's fall on the stairs until Mary had come running in to tell her there was an ambulance down there taking him away to the hospital and him swearing something awful, not that you could blame the poor man.

'And herself wanting tea on the dot of five as usual, and me in the midst of boning a chicken and I couldn't even go to see them carrying him off,' Cook lamented.

Herself considered Mr Kelling to have been struck down by a Mighty Hand, and it a judgment upon him for his riotous and ungodly ways. Cook and Mary, however, thought Mr Kelling was a lovely man, always so friendly and kind-spoken when he happened to meet one of them, which wasn't often because herself was a lady of the old school and believed in servants using the back stairs.

This very night, mind you, Mary had been made to go out through the alley and walk clear back around the block to meet the taxi at the kerb, while herself went down in the elevator. Mary would most likely get to use the front stairs when they got back, though, it being late by then and good maids hard to come by.

'Does your employer ever climb the stairs?' Max asked.

'Herself? Not so's you'd notice it. If the elevator gets stuck, it's me or Mary that has to go find it and send it up to her. Could I cut you another sliver of cake, maybe?'

'Thanks, but I'm afraid we ought to be going. Egbert has to get some things ready for my wife to take to Mr Kelling tomorrow morning '

'Would he fancy a piece of my cake, do you think?'

'Only if you baked a bottle of Old Granddad in the middle of it,' said Egbert, and they parted on a merry note.

As they went downstairs, Egbert asked, 'What is it you want me to pack for Mrs Sarah?'

'Nothing, actually,' Max told him. 'I just thought we'd better get out of there before herself showed up and we had to sneak down the back stairs. What I really want from you is a picture of that Codfish thing. Jem said he'd show me one. Would you know where to get hold of it?'

'Easiest thing in the world, Mr Max. Mr Jem has a whole scrapbook, right from the time he first joined the Comrades of the Convivial Codfish. It's one of his dearest possessions, next to the feather from Ann Corio's dove and the tassel off Sally Keith's—er—costume.'

'Trust Jem to keep his priorities straight. Where's the scrapbook?'

New Englanders are notorious for their addiction to

photograph albums  Egbert was only too pleased to display Jem's treasure, and Max showed a gratifying interest. After studying the photographs, he detached two of them: a recent picture of the entire group and a close-up of Jem with the Great Chain adorning his well-padded front

'I'll take these along with me '

Egbert was alarmed 'Mr Max, if anything should happen to those photos, Mr Jem would have a stroke '

'I'll guard them with my life  Where's his invitation to the Tolbathys' party?'

'It's a ticket. Mr Tolbathy had them printed up special Can't ride the train without a ticket, you know  Just a second.'

Egbert went and got the strip of cardboard off Jem's dresser. 'Is it a clue, do you think?'

'Who knows? At any rate, Jem won't be using it  Why let it go to waste? Sleep tight, Egbert  And stay off those stairs One broken hip in the family is plenty '

In fact it was more than plenty, as Sarah and Max found out the next morning when they went to call on their fallen relative  Max really didn't have the time to spare for hospital visits, but he entertained a reasonable scepticism about accidents caused by wax on stairways, power outages that occurred in second-floor flats and not on the floor above, and urgent telephone calls prompting the consequent victim to rush out and do what he would not otherwise have done.

They found Jem propped up in bed, howling for brandy and being told by an exasperated nurse to suck the alcohol off the thermometer  Sarah noticed the nurse was keeping well out of pinching range. She herself approached the bed boldly  Nipping nieces, however temptingly they might be constructed, was not Jeremy Kelling's idea of fun.

'Shut up, you old satyr,' she told him affectionately 'I've brought you an eggnog, which is more than you deserve. Did you eat your breakfast?'

'Faugh! Barging in here and poking porridge at me in the

middle of the night Of course I didn't eat it Think I'm going to truckle to petticoat despotism at my time of life? What are you two doing here at this ungodly hour?'

'It's half past ten and Max wants to detect you '

'Oh About time. Where the hell's my Codfish?'

Jem snarled venomously at a small plastic gnome some would-be bringer of light had stuck on his bed table, and swigged his eggnog Somewhat pacified, he allowed Max to grill him about the alleged accident on the stairs

About the events leading up to it, his account was identical to Egbert's He seemed not to realize he'd skidded on wax, though All he knew was that his feet had flown out from under him and he'd landed at the bottom with a busted backside There was no way he could blame Max Bittersohn for what happened, but it was obvious he'd have liked to.

Max refused to be intimidated 'Now, about those false whiskers Did you mention to anybody other than Egbert that you were getting them from Fuzzleys'?'

'Where the hell else would I get them? Answer me that '

'Jack's Joke Shop?'

'Blah! I wanted whiskers with class and dignity, not a goddamn Groucho Marx moustache with a false nose hitched on to it. You don't get class and dignity at Jack's You get plastic vomit and whoopee cushions. Not that I haven't thrown a fair amount of business their way over the years, mind you, and not that I haven't found their products entirely satisfactory for the purposes to which they were put.'

'They'll be grateful for the endorsement, I'm sure Getting back to Fuzzleys', you've dealt with them before? They know you, do they?'

'I wouldn't necessarily go so far as to say they know me. I mean, what the hell, a man doesn't go buying a new set of false whiskers every day in the week, does he?'

'But you did place an order with them?'

'Not precisely, if you have to be precise. What I did was, I called them up and asked if they happened to have any dundreary whiskers in a rich chestnut brown tone The chap who answered said he was sure they could accommodate me and why didn't I buzz over and take a look, or words to that effect '

'When was this?'

'Sometime last week, I suppose. I forget the exact day '

'Did you then go to the shop?'

'No,' Jem confessed, 'I forgot that, too. Damn it, I had more important things on my mind at the time '

'Then how do you suppose the person who called knew who you were?'

Jem stuck out his pink little lower lip in a Churchillian manner and pondered 'Good question. I must have assumed I'd given it when I called them in the first place The thing is, first I'd been preoccupied with Scrooge Day, then I'd been worried about losing the Codfish One way and another, I hadn't given much thought to the Tolbathys' shindig. When that chap called, I was so glad to be re-minded, I just grabbed my coat and whizzed on out I thought I'd better get those whiskers right away, before I forgot again and wound up on the train with my bare face hanging out. Anything else you want to know?'

'Yes, why dundrearies? I thought Jay Gould wore a walrus moustache '

'So what? Every blasted male at the party will be wearing a walrus moustache Bunch of unimaginative clods. My rationale was that Jay Gould would have worn dundreary whiskers instead of a walrus moustache if he'd had superior taste and savoir faire I was going to represent an idealization of Jay Gould. It was an uplifting thought, and look where it got me. I must remember to throw that up to Mabel the next time she comes yammering at me about leading a purer and nobler life. God, Sarah, you haven't told Mabel I'm in the hospital? Or Appie? If Appie finds out, she'll be over here at six o'clock every morning, trying to make me eat that porridge.'

'Relax, Uncle Jem. You know perfectly well Cousin Mabel always goes away for the holidays so she won't have to give any of the relatives a present. And Aunt Appie's up in Vermont with her son Lionel, shopping for a ski lodge. Lionel thought it would be nice if she surprised his wife and children with one as a Christmas present. He's being awfully helpful about finding ways for her to spend all that money she inherited before she dies and sticks him with the inheritance tax I expect Cousin Theonia will be over later on to soothe your fevered brow, but you know you'll adore that.'

'Ah, yes. When I muse upon what might have been.' Jem mused for approximately three seconds on the voluptuous beauty his Cousin Brooks had wooed away with heroic deeds and exotic birdcalls. Then he started up, cursed the pain in his hip, and fell back.

'Make them bring me a telephone, quick. Somebody's got to call Marcia Whet and break the news that I can't be her escort tonight, damn it. Poor woman, she'll have to settle for old Wripp.'

'No she won't,' said Max. 'I'm hurling myself into the breach. Don't glare at me like that, Sarah. I don't even know the woman, for God's sake. I'll probably have a terrible time.'

'Not at all,' Jem was tactless enough to assure him. 'Marcia's a great gal. Perfectly respectable and so forth, but always ready for a—oh, very well, Sarah. I was only trying to perk up Max's morale.'

'I'll attend to Max's morale, thank you. Get some rest and keep your hands off the nurses. Egbert will be along pretty soon, I expect.'

'He'd damn well better be. I want a shave.'

Jeremy Kelling gave the plastic gnome another dirty look, then closed his eyes in pious resignation. 'Be kind to her, Max. With all her faults, I love her still.'

His niece sniffed. 'Her whom? Me or Mrs Whet? Come on, Max. These affecting deathbed scenes tend to lose their poignancy if they're allowed to drag on too long.'

## CHAPTER 4

'What's your programme for today?' Max asked as they walked up towards Washington Street together

'I thought I'd stop in at Jordan's and see what I can find for Miriam,' Sarah told him. 'Maybe something rather elegant in the way of cookware She'd like that, wouldn't she?'

'She'll like whatever you give her For God's sake, Sarah, you don't have to knock yourself out trying to please my family. We've never made a big deal over the holidays.'

'Darling, please remember they're my family now, too. If you can be so noble and self-sacrificing about leaving me home and taking Marcia Whet to a lovely party, the least I can do is buy your sister a new teakettle.'

God, women could be maddening. What was a man supposed to say to that? Nothing, probably Max played safe by pulling out his wallet

'Need any money?'

'I expect so Thank you, darling. Where are you off to?'

'Fuzzleys' I want to ask them about that phone call Jem claims they made '

'Then I'll see you back at the apartment.'

They went their respective ways. As Max had expected, nobody at Fuzzleys' admitted to having made such a call

'Why should we?' the manager asked him 'Look at this ' He pulled out a long drawer filled with beards and moustaches in every possible shade of design 'And this, and this, and this '

He seemed ready to go on slamming drawers and waving beards indefinitely, but Max conceded the point. There was simply no reason why Fuzzleys' would have to fuss about special orders.

'We just tell them to come in,' said the manager. 'If we don't have what they want, which isn't likely, we take some crepe hair, like this ' He selected false hair of a shade to match Max's own, and proceeded to fashion a pair of superb side-whiskers and a natty little moustache.

Max was fascinated. He liked seeing anything done well. And there was a theatrical streak in him, though he tried to pretend there wasn't, that revelled in an excuse to get himself up as an Edwardian masher. When he showed them off to Sarah later, he looked so wickedly dashing she could hardly stand to let him go off without her.

'I'm going over and cry on Cousin Theonia's shoulder,' was her valediction. 'Here, don't forget your silk hat. I just hope Marcia Whet appreciates what she's getting '

'So do I '

Max was having a touch of stage fright, but he needn't have fretted When he arrived at the Whet house in a cab he'd picked up at the corner of Beacon and Charles, he found Mrs Whet waiting for him at the door, goggle-eyed So was the elderly maid standing behind her with a fur-lined pelisse at the ready

As he doffed his top hat and remarked, 'It was kind of you to let me come in Jem's place,' Mrs Whet chuckled.

'My dear man, I feel as if I've cast my bread on the waters and got back *bûche de Noël*. I'd love to ask you in for a tête-à-tête and scandalize the household, but I'm afraid we ought to be getting along or we'll miss our train. My cloak, please, Maria Mr Bittersohn, do you really think we can get me and all these clothes into that one little cab?'

Max wasn't too sure Marcia Whet was, as he'd antici-pated, a fine figure of a woman Twelve yards of skirt, a bustle, God knew how many petticoats, the fur-lined pelisse, a foxtail boa, and a matching muff the size of a sofa pillow, topped off with a hat wide enough to support a whole stuffed pheasant, which in fact it was doing, did not tend to minimize the lady's contours. It took a fair amount of manoeuvring and a few discreet shoves to get her stowed inside, but neither her finery nor her temper got ruffled in the process. By the time they got to North Station, she was calling him Max and he was beginning to feel that an evening without Sarah might be supportable after all.

At trackside, they found a number of the Tolbathys' other guests, all in suitable costumes and great spirits, waiting to board the regrettably modern Buddliner that was to take them on the first stage of their journey. Marcia Whet plunged in among them, towing Max by the hand and introducing him right and left as her dear, dear friend Mr Jay Gould. He got more puzzled glances than acknowledgments People must either be wondering where they'd seen him before or else making mental notes to have a quiet chat with Mr Whet when he got back from Nairobi.

Max in turn was trying to sort out the Comrades of the Convivial Codfish and finding it an uphill swim. While studying the group photo earlier, he'd noticed these piscatorial pals were better described as birds of a feather who actually did prefer to flock together. They must all have been lined up and stamped out with the same cookie cutter, he thought gloomily Furthermore, as Jem had predicted, practically all of them were wearing enormous handlebar moustaches. That must have been good for Fuzzleys' business, but it wasn't going to be so great for Bittersohn's Once they got their overcoats off and appeared in conventional evening dress, as no doubt they would, he might as well try to detect a flock of penguins.

Well, maybe he'd get them sorted out after a while. They didn't appear to be having any difficulty recognizing one another. Probably penguins didn't either.

As for himself, it was not to be imagined that a bunch of

Yankees who'd no doubt been nesting in each other's family trees for generations would settle for any persiflage about Jay Gould. Marcia Whet was now explaining that her escort was in fact poor darling Jeremy Kelling's nephew Max, who'd been hurled into the breach opened by Jem's dreadful accident. She described Jem's downfall with verve and inaccuracy, drawing cries of compassion from some and derision from others. The latter group, Max decided, must be those Comrades who hadn't yet got over the effects of their Scrooge Day celebration.

The scoffers at least gave him a starting point. He pegged Comrade Durward easily on account of his thick eyeglasses and Comrade Wripp from his two canes and general air of advanced decrepitude. He was by now fairly sure of Comrade Dork and Comrade Billingsgate. These were both neighbours of the Tolbathys who'd had themselves chauffeured to Boston, moustaches and all, just so they could ride back again on the train.

Max identified Comrade Ogham from the fact that one of the moustaches was giving him the cold shoulder; and was amused to realize it had to be on account of his alleged relationship to Jem. The Kelling clan was so vast and bewildering that nobody so far had tried to pinpoint just where Max fitted in. It was a novelty to be snubbed as a Kelling instead of as a Bittersohn

There weren't many nonpartying riders on the train, and that was probably a good thing. Those who didn't belong to the Tolbathy group were clearly nonplussed by this invasion of Edwardians. The really confusing thing was that so many of the Codfish and their Codesses were old enough to look as if they belonged in the clothes they were wearing.

Despite their accumulated longevity, they were a lively bunch. There was far too much aisle-hopping and seat-switching to help Max compile his personal Who's Who. He'd hoped Marcia Whet would clue him in, but she was fully occupied being the life of the party. At last Max gave up and just sat looking handsome and inscrutable until the conductor came through chanting, 'Lincoln Station '

What with all the bustles and boas and dropped gloves and misplaced derbies, it took them quite a while to disembark At last they were every last one of them out in the biting night and there, sure enough, was a bright red bus lit up like a Christmas tree with the driver passing out glasses of champagne to make sure nobody got carsick on the ride to the Tolbathys'. Max hoped to God the driver himself wasn't having any Neither was he, though he'd taken a glass from the tray when the rest did because it would have looked too eccentric for a nephew of Jeremy Kelling's not to

They had a lot more snow out here than in the city It made Max think of the woods up at Ireson's Landing and wish he and Sarah were back there in the old carriage house raising each other's thermal coefficient As the champagne went down and the party revved up, he wished so with yet more fervour. Why had he thought it would be a good idea to involve himself in this geriatric saturnalia?

Because, he told himself angrily, it really was a good idea. Jeremy Kelling had damn near got himself murdered, and Max wanted to know why Jem wasn't rich enough to get killed for his money. His philandering, such as it was these days, was hardly of the sort to inflame a husband or lover to murderous rage. Jem wasn't innocent enough to be anybody's dupe or wise enough to be anybody's nemesis. The only logical explanation for that waxed staircase and the faked telephone call that lured him down it was that somebody'd been desperately concerned to keep Jeremy Kelling from attending the Tolbathys' party.

Or maybe it wasn't the only logical explanation. Where did that missing chain with the silver codfish on it come in? Max must have become lost in cogitation, for Marcia Whet reached over to tickle his nose with one of her foxtails.

'Darling Mr Gould, you're not leaving us yet, surely? Not

on one silly little glass of champagne? The evening hasn't even begun.'

Max opened his eyes and smiled, causing his moustache to twitch beguilingly though he hadn't intended it to. 'Oh no. I was only thinking about poor old Jem. He's going to come down with apoplexy when I tell him what he's missed.'

Marcia laughed. 'They must be having to tie him to the bed. I shouldn't be a whit surprised to see him come charging down the track after us in a wheelchair with his johnny strung up on his crutches for a sail Only Jem wouldn't be wearing anything so prosaic as a hospital johnny, would he? A lovely red-and-white nightshirt would be more his speed, and a cap with a tassel wagging in the wind. Can't you just see him?'

She did have a charming laugh. 'I'm going to miss Jem terribly tonight, with all respect to your gallant self. You see, I'm much too vain to wear my eyeglasses out in company, so I never know who's who unless Jem keeps me informed. He has eyesight like an eagle, you know.'

'I never realized that,' said Max.

'Oh, my stars, yes. It's Jem's great talent. He can spot the vaguest acquaintance half a mile away. I don't know how he does it, but he remembers every least little thing. You know, such as people's having one ear higher than the other or walking with their toes turned in. All those ridiculous details most of us never even notice. And he knows absolutely everybody, though half the time he isn't speaking to them. You should see him snooting Obed Ogham.'

'Is that Ogham in the grey top hat and yellow gloves?'

'My dear man, didn't I just this moment tell you I'm blind as a bat? Wait till Obed comes within range of my lorgnette and I'll point him out to you.'

'Thanks. I ought to know, for the sake of family unity. Any snoot of Jem's is a snoot of mine. Tonight, at any rate. That's interesting about Jem's ability to recognize people at a distance. Do many of his friends know he can do it?'

'Heavens, yes, we all do. That's why Jem's so indispens-able at parties. One's always sidling up to him and whisper-ing, 'Who's that hideous woman in the purple dress?' or whatever. He saves us no end of embarrassment since the woman's apt to be one's own sister-in-law. Or ex-sister-in-law, which could be even stickier.'

'I can see where it might be.'

And right there was an excellent reason why Jem might have had to be kept away from the Tolbathys' party at any cost. Somebody, not necessarily in this particular contingent but among those who'd be on the train in the course of the evening, didn't want to risk being recognized by the one person who'd be able to see through his or her disguise.

Max rather inclined towards a him The women had altered the style of their clothing, though perhaps not very much in some instances, but there wasn't a great deal they could do about their faces. The men, on the other hand, had a glorious excuse to mask their features behind unaccustomed hirsute adornments.

False beards and wigs were traditionally effective dis-guises. This crowd was surely as tradition-oriented as they came. From what Marcia Whet said about their general acuity of vision, most of them could probably be fooled by a wad or two of Fuzzleys' best so long as the person behind it didn't get too close or talk too much. Or at least the prankster would assume they could.

As to whether there was in fact such a plot in the works, Max would know soon enough. He did wish he weren't so handicapped by being the lone stranger here. Some of the guests were married couples, of course, and he could have recognized the husbands through their wives if only he knew the wives. The age level being what it was, though, there must be a fair percentage of widows and widowers, along with those few who'd never married at all. He wasn't too sanguine about his own chances of getting them sorted out in time to spot an odd one. Marcia Whet was not going to help

him much. He'd have to forgo her amiable company and
attach himself to somebody who could see past her lorgnette.

That should be feasible. Now that they knew who Max
was, or thought they did, even the men were friendly enough.
The one he'd recognized as Durward kept leaning across the
aisle to chat, squinting amiably up at him through those
bottle-bottom spectacles. The hitch there was that Durward
had mistaken Max for a tenor named Ernest who used to sing
madrigals with him, whereas Max was a baritone who sang
things like 'They're hanging Danny Deever in the morning,'
and then only when he was shaving or putting on his socks.
Durward was clearly another lost cause.

Obed Ogham could be scratched at the post, naturally. He
was making a great point of not noticing Jeremy Kelling's
nephew, though sneaking frequent glances to make sure Max
realized he was being ignored. Max wondered how many of
the others wished they could be ignored, too. Ogham was the
sort of man who backs people into corners and shouts funny
stories at them regardless of their protests that they've
already heard the jokes and didn't think they were any good
the first time. Max felt a glow of family pride at Jeremy
Kelling's taste and discrimination in being on the outs with
Ogham, as well as a sense of relief at being exempt from
getting pounded at by that loud, arrogant voice.

The bus ride seemed to be taking one hell of a long time,
although Max's watch told him it wasn't. He was relieved
when at last they turned off the road, up a well-ploughed
private drive. For perhaps an eighth of a mile he saw only
snow-covered trees, then an expanse of clear snow that must
be lawn. Then everybody began exclaiming, 'There it is!
There's the train.'

And there it was, dwarfed by the vast mansion on the hill
behind it but ablaze with light, sitting self-importantly on its
loop of track outside a miniature station festooned with
Christmas greens. Beside the step, a lavishly uniformed
conductor made a great play with a nickel-plated stem-

winder watch and yelled, 'Boo-ard! All aboard. Step lively, please.'

That was Tom Tolbathy, their host. His wife stood inside the parlour car, greeting each guest as they climbed up. Mrs Tolbathy was doing a marvellous imitation of Margaret Dumont, Max thought, wearing silver lace over a straight-front corset, with white kid gloves up to her armpits and strings of pearls down to her knees. She didn't seem to be having any difficulty figuring out who was who despite the moustaches, though she did look the merest trifle nonplussed when Max Bittersohn took off his top hat and made his bow.

'This is Jeremy Kelling's nephew Max, Hester,' Marcia Whet explained for about the fifteenth time so far. 'Poor Jem broke his hip last night, so he dragooned Max into being my escort '

'How dreadful,' said Hester Tolbathy. 'Not you, Max. I may call you that, mayn't I? You were a darling to pitch in, and we're delighted to have you aboard Which branch of the Kellings do you perch on?'

Max started to explain that he was only a graft, but just then Tom Tolbathy boosted old Mr Wripp up on the steps, so Hester had to turn and inquire about all the eldest Comrade's ailments, from the cataracts in his eyes to the gout in his toes That was clearly going to take a while, so Max let himself be swept on with Marcia Whet through the parlour car, with its ornate gilt and crimson damask decor, into what might once have been a coal tender. This was now converted into a sort of utility area, with a brass and mahogany coat rack along the wall and a potbellied stove in the middle throwing an almost insufferable amount of heat.

A pretty child of twelve or so in a long velvet dress with a lace collar was there to take coats She turned out to be the Tolbathys' granddaughter, showed her matching lace pan-talettes to Marcia Whet, who must be an intimate family friend, lamented that she was going to be kicked off and sent to bed before the train started, and finally got around to hanging up Max's black cashmere overcoat and stowing the pop-top hat Dolph's wife, Mary, had resurrected originally for Jem to wear Together, she and Max got Mrs Whet out of her boa, pelisse, and pheasant; then Max escorted the elder lady back against the rising tide of petticoats and pseudo-pelage.

The Tolbathys knew how to put on an elegant affair, that was clear. The lights were dim enough to make all the ladies look handsome and all the men at least moderately distinguished. Max saw no fountain spouting champagne—that must have been one of the flights of hyperbole to which Uncle Jem was so prone—but he did observe a bar set up in the dining car, manned by a bartender wearing red arm garters, the inevitable walrus moustache with well-waxed ends, and a black toupee neatly parted down the middle. Beside the bar stood a square table draped in white damask, bearing an elaborate silver epergne topped by a swan carved out of ice It was the sort of thing that ought to have dishes of food on it, but there was not a bite of anything in sight, and that surprised Max a great deal.

Somebody else must have been thinking along the same line, for Max heard a man behind him mutter, 'For God's sake, aren't they going to feed us?'

'Be patient, dear,' said the woman who was presumably his wife. 'You know Hester always does things in grand style. I expect the caterers are a little late getting organized '

'Caterers? Why couldn't they have used their own staff?'

'To serve a crowd like this on a moving train? Darling, Hester knows better even then to suggest it. Oh, goody, more champagne.'

Over at the table beside the bar, a wine steward, correct in black coat, white gloves, and a heavy silver chain of office with a silver corkscrew dangling from it, was deftly easing the cork out of a magnum. Max went over to get some for Marcia Whet and took a long, thoughtful look at the silver chain while he was waiting for the bubbly to be poured.

The sommelier paid no attention to Max or to anybody else but filled glasses in dignified silence until the bottle was empty. Then he opened another magnum from the ice-filled silver bucket that stood on the bar. Then he handed the duty of pouring over to the bartender and disappeared.

Almost immediately he was back, carrying a biggish silver tray. He busied himself about the epergne for a moment or two, then stood back so those clustered around the bar could see the effect he'd achieved The upper arms were now laden with cut-glass dishes of chopped onion, sieved egg yolk, and curls of sweet butter; the lower ones with silver baskets of thin-sliced dark bread and crisp melba toast.

'Now he's going to open the caviar,' Marcia Whet murmured to Max over the top of her champagne glass. 'The Tolbathys always make a thing of the caviar Tom imports it, you know.'

'I didn't, actually. What else does he import?'

'Escargots, marrons glacés, that sort of thing Tom's Fancy Foreign Foods. Tom and his brother Wouter, I should say; though *entre nous*, Tom's the driving force now that their father is gone. I do wish that man would get on with it. I adore caviar.'

However, the man with the silver chain took his time, scrutinizing the tin for any possible flaw, then inserting the tip of a handheld can opener and painstakingly screwing it around until the lid came off clean. He held the opened tin up for yet another inspection, then carefully scooped its contents out with a silver spoon into a gleaming crystal bowl. At last, like a Mayan priest offering up a virgin, he lifted the bowl in both hands, placed it in the hollowed-out back of the carved ice swan, picked up his tray now bearing only the used can opener and the emptied tin, and stepped through the vestibule from the dining car to the caboose, from which the serving was evidently being done.

A waitress who'd been hovering in the background now stepped up to the table and began spreading the sweet butter on the bread and toast, spooning out the expensive fish eggs, adding sprinkles of egg yolk or onion, and laying them on a tray for another waitress to pass among the guests. Max didn't care much for caviar, so he shook his head when the tray got to him. Marcia Whet was aghast.

'You horrid man, how could you?'

'Sorry, I just don't happen to like it.'

'But you could have taken one anyway, and slipped it to me. Then I'd get more than my fair share without looking quite so piggish.'

As a rule, nobody eats much caviar because it is so rich. Either because the Tolbathys' was such a special kind, though, or because there still wasn't anything else being served, the bowl emptied quickly. People were going up to the table and manufacturing their own appetizers Max rather expected the man with the chain to come back and refill the swan, but he didn't. Instead, one of the waitresses took the empty dishes from the epergne and went off, Max hoped, to get some hors d'oeuvres that were more to his taste He was feeling hungry.

He was also feeling the motion of the train as he had not done before. They'd speeded up, for some reason. Passengers who'd been balancing themselves easily against the gentle rocking of the cars were grabbing frantically at anything they could hang on to Hester Tolbathy looked startled, Tom Tolbathy furious He set down the drink he'd been sipping and started forward Max forgot about food and moved to follow Tom

That was when the train stopped, so abruptly that bottles and glasses went flying off the bar. The great silver epergne slid off its table; the swan splintered into icy fragments. Passengers crashed to the floor. Tom Tolbathy turned and hesitated, clearly torn between duty to his guests and concern for his train.

The train won. Tom hurried through the parlour car, through the coal tender where, mercifully, the potbellied stove had not fallen over and started a fire He either didn't notice or didn't care that Max Bittersohn was right with him; but wrenched open a connecting door and stuck his head into the engine cab.

'Wouter, what the hell—'

Tom Tolbathy didn't say any more. His brother was not at the controls He was huddled, face down, into the tiny space on the floor of the cab.


## CHAPTER 5

'Oh my God, Wouter! Hey, old fellow, what's the matter?'

Tom Tolbathy was down on the floor beside his brother, pulling his body half-upright, slapping at his cheeks, trying to bully him back to consciousness Max noted the lolling head, the half-open eyes and mouth, and put a hand on Tom's shoulder to make him stop

'I'm afraid he's not going to wake up, Tom '

'What do you mean? What's the matter with him?'

'I think he's dead. Let me down there a second, will you?'

Tom shifted Max took his place beside the fallen engineer After a little fumbling, he shook his head

'I can't find any sign of life Did your brother have heart trouble, do you know?'

'Wouter? Never Sound as a bell At least he always said he was Damn it all,' Tolbathy's face screwed up as if he wanted to cry, 'he can't be dead.'

All Max could say was, 'We'd better get a doctor How far are we from the house?'

Tom shook his head, as if to get his brain started. 'I'll have to find out where we are. It's so damned dark out here—'

He took a battery lantern from a hook behind the control panel and leaned out the cab window. Max bent over Wouter Tolbathy again. Considering that he held his doctorate in fine arts rather than medicine, he knew a surprising lot about dead bodies Wouter's was that, no doubt about it

He might have died as a result of that sudden jolting stop, if he'd got thrown back against the iron plates of the cab wall But he hadn't. There was no wound on the back of his head, no bleeding from the mouth or nostrils. What this looked like was one of those wartime movies where the commando climbs into the locomotive, gives the engineer a quick chop across the hyoid bone with the heel of his hand, and takes over the train Max's previous experience hadn't run to hyoid bones, but it did look to him as if Wouter Tolbathy's Adam's apple had an awfully ominous dent in it

He thought he wouldn't say so just yet to Tom Tolbathy The brother was having all he could do to function rationally as it was Tom looked like death himself when he pulled his head back into the cab

'We're right at the far end of the loop, about two miles from the house '

'Is there any place near here where we could make a phone call?'

'No, it's all conservation land I'll have to take her back to the station That's the closest phone Let's hope to God she still runs '

As Tom turned to the instrument panel, he stumbled over his dead brother's body. Max thought he was going to faint

'We've got to get Wouter out of here. Take his feet, will you, Max? We'll stretch him out in the tender and cover him with a tablecloth till—'

'I don't think we ought to move him, Tom,' Max had to answer.

'For God's sake, why not? I can't stand to leave him like this. It isn't decent Oh Christ, how did this have to happen?'

'It looks to me as if we'll have to take that question up with the police.'

'What do you mean? Why should a heart attack have anything to do with them?'

'You always call the police in a case like this Besides, I'm afraid it wasn't a heart attack. His windpipe's been smashed.'

'His windpipe? You mean—but how could that happen? Unless he got dizzy or something and slammed on the brakes too fast and the jolt—'

'The jolt could have killed him, I'll grant you that. I'd much rather believe it had, if only he'd got a cut on his forehead, or a bloody nose, or even a black eye. But I'm damned if I can see anything in this cab that could have dealt him a clean swipe across the throat and not left him with so much as a scratch on his chin. It's far more likely, in my opinion, that he was dead before the train stopped, and I'm afraid we're going to get into even worse trouble than we are now if we move the body before the police get a chance to see it.'

Tolbathy looked at Bittersohn for a moment without speaking Then he nodded, leaned over his dead brother's body in an awkward stoop, and reached for the starting lever.

'Wouter?' Somebody was trying to get into the cab 'Wouter, are you there?'

'I'm here,' said Tom. 'What is it, Quent?'

The door opened and a head appeared. 'Hester sent me to find out what's happening. Some of the passengers got shaken up, and she thinks old Wripp may have broken something. What shall I tell her?'

'Tell her Wouter's had a—an accident, and we're going back to the house to call a doctor '

'What happened to you, Wouter?' This was the man in the thick glasses who'd thought back on the bus that Max was his madrigal-singing acquaintance Ernest. Max glanced at Tolbathy for a cue.

'Let him alone, Quent,' Tom obliged him by saying. 'He's still stunned. I believe he saw a deer on the track, braked too abruptly, and banged his head. We've had problems with them this year. I only hope the engine isn't damaged. Make sure nobody else comes in here, will you? I—want Wouter to get some rest.'

Durward said, 'Of course,' and disappeared Tolbathy threw the starting switch. The engine came alive instantly. They moved along the track for twenty feet or so, then slowed down and came to a full stop.

'What's the matter?' asked Max.

'Nothing, thank God I wanted to test the brakes before I put on speed. It could have been a deer, you know.' Tolbathy's voice was almost pleading. 'We should have looked for tracks in the snow '

'Wouldn't you have noticed them when you looked out back there to get your bearings?'

Tolbathy didn't answer, just started the train again. Max decided it was time to come clean.

'Look, Tom, I'd better explain why I'm here. The thing is, I'm not exactly Jem Kelling's nephew I'm his niece Sarah's husband. My name is Max Bittersohn and I'm a private investigator by profession. The reason I crashed your party tonight is that Jem's so-called accident was an elaborately rigged attempt to murder or disable him. Whoever fixed the trap didn't seem to care which, and the only explanation I can think of is that somebody didn't want him on this train tonight.'

'But why? What could Jem's not being here have to do with Wouter's—getting killed?'

'Possibly a great deal. Offhand, I can think of two reasons why Jem might have to be kept away. For one, Jem has an unusual faculty for being able to recognize even casual acquaintances.'

'That's right, he does. But we're not casual acquaintances here. We're all old friends.'

'Are we? What about the bartender, or the waitresses? What about me, if it comes to that? You accepted me at face value because I came with your friend Marcia Whet and was introduced as Jem Kelling's nephew. In fact, she'd never met me before tonight, and didn't even have her facts straight. I showed up in a taxi, told her Jem had sent me to bring her to the party, and she believed me because she wanted to. You see how easy it could be to crash a party?'

'But my wife and I greeted everyone personally.'

'Did you? There was a crush when we all piled off the bus at the same time and hurried to get on the train because it was cold outside Inevitably, some of your guests received more attention than others Mr Wripp, for instance. You helped him up the steps and your wife made a big fuss over him, as people naturally do with someone so old If somebody had squeezed past while you were getting Wripp settled, you'd have been too busy to stop and shake hands or whatever If you didn't quite recognize the person, you'd have assumed it was because he or she was in costume, if you thought about it at all '

'I suppose such a thing could have happened,' Tolbathy admitted, 'but I can't recall that it did '

'That's my whole point You wouldn't have noticed But Jem Kelling would Furthermore, Jem would have been sure to spot his own ceremonial chain of office, or whatever the hell you call that codfish thing he lost at your meeting yesterday.'

'The Great Chain? Why do you bring that up?'

'Because that man who brought out the caviar was wearing it tonight '

'What man? Oh, you mean the wine steward Nonsense, Bittersohn That was merely someone from the caterers It's quite customary, you know, for sommeliers to wear such chains '

'Not such chains as that one. The codfish pendant had been removed and a silver corkscrew put in its place, but the chain itself was identical to the one Jem assumed when he took office Take my word for it, Tom It's a superb and I should say almost unique piece of craftsmanship. Stolen jewelry happens to be one of my specialities, and I have an excellent eye for detail.'

'Oh, now I've placed you. You're the man who got involved with young Sarah over that business of the Kelling rubies. I didn't realize she'd married you.'

Tolbathy's tone was now carefully polite. Even straddling his dead brother's body to get at the controls, he couldn't forget who he was and who Bittersohn was. Sarah complained that she got the same kind of treatment from Max's mother.

'I'm afraid I don't at all understand what you're driving at,' he went on 'Why should some stranger sneak into the party and put on the Great Chain to murder my brother? Why would anybody kill my brother?' Brusquely, Tom Tolbathy cleared his throat. 'Wouter was the gentlest chap imaginable He hadn't an enemy in the world. That sounds trite, but it's true of Wouter. Believe me, I'd have known Wouter and I have always been,' his voice quivered again, 'very close '

It was hateful having to badger the man at a time like this, but Max persisted. 'Did he live near you?'

'With us, actually Wouter never married. Never did much of anything, I suppose, when you come right down to it, except putter around and play with his trains. But Wouter was a happy soul. It was enough, just having him around. When the children were young he'd tell them stories, take them for walks in the woods, teach them to run the trains God, how am I going to tell them?'

That was Tom's problem, not Max Bittersohn's 'I understand your brother was in business with you.'

'Yes As a matter of fact, he was.' Tolbathy sounded somewhat surprised to be reminded.

'What was his position in the firm?'

'That's rather a hard one to answer. Ours is a smallish family concern, you know We don't go in for organization

charts. Wouter's official title was vice-president, but he liked
to dabble in this and that. He'd simply drift around and lend
a hand where one was needed.'

Sorted the mail and unpacked the chocolate Santa
Clauses, no doubt. Max had done business with old family
firms before, and he'd never yet found one that didn't have a
Wouter or two on the payroll. They were often incompetent,
sometimes nuisances, but seldom such festering thorns that
they became targets for elaborate and risky murder plots. By
and large, Wouter Tolbathy sounded like an improbable
victim. But there he lay, huddled at his brother's feet with an
expertly broken neck. Did his being Wouter Tolbathy have
anything to do with his being killed? If not, what was the
point?

In the movies, the engineer got scragged because either the
good guys or the bad guys needed the train to take them
somewhere for some noble or nefarious purpose, depending
on which side they belonged to But this train didn't go
anywhere and appeared to have no purpose, except to
provide an expensive source of amusement for the Tolbathys
and their friends. It hardly seemed likely some Comrade of
the Convivial Codfish had got so caught up in the spirit of
Scrooge Day that he'd nobbled the Exalted Chowderhead
and assassinated the brother of Marley's Ghost just to
provide a dramatic windup to their Christmas party. Max
sighed and went on asking questions.

'Who, other than yourself and your brother, would know
how to operate this train?'

'Almost anybody, with a little instruction,' Tom Tolbathy
replied. 'These controls are elementary, really. Wouter and I
would have preferred a real old steam-driven locomotive, but
it simply wasn't practical. They take so long to fire up, you
know. Then you've got the smoke and the mess from the coal
and the danger of sparks setting fire to the woods, not to
mention the shovelling. That means a two-man crew, which
is no good if one of us wants—wanted—to take her out

single-handed. So we compromised by having this one built. It looks like an old-timer but runs on batteries, actually. That's why we have space behind the cab for a cloakroom or what have you We stuck in that old potbellied stove to provide atmosphere and manufacture some real smoke for the smokestack. Silly make-believe, I suppose, but there it is.'

He reached over and fiddled with one of the switches. 'Most of our friends have taken a shot at running her one time or another.'

'So in fact,' said Max, 'that quick speedup and jolting stop could have been engineered by whoever had entered the cab and killed your brother.'

'Oh yes, no problem. You could do it yourself, I expect, just from watching me. Now that you've mentioned it, I expect that was what happened. Wouter wasn't the type to play nasty practical jokes, especially when we had guests aboard. He was never much for parties himself, but he knew how eager Hester was to have everything go with a swing. I couldn't think why he'd pull such a stunt on purpose. Oh, God, if I'd only come forward sooner! If I hadn't lost my balance when we stopped short—'

'Who didn't?' Max reminded him. 'That could be why it was done, to give the killer a chance to escape while we were all trying to pull ourselves together. After we've got the passengers unloaded and the rest of it taken care of, it mightn't be a bad idea to come back out to the place where we stopped and check around for footprints in the snow.'

'I dare say I can find someone to run the train for you ' Tolbathy was still polite but sounded desperately tired 'I doubt whether I myself will be free to do it. Aside from everything else, nobody's had any dinner yet and the passengers will have to be got home one way or another. People didn't bring their own cars, and I don't suppose anyone will feel like trekking back via Lincoln Station. By the way, didn't

Quent say something about Wripp's being rather badly hurt?'

'Yes, he did Quent is Comrade Durward, right? He seems to be under the impression we're old buddies, but I don't recall having met him before.'

'He's confused you with somebody else, that's all Quent's eyes are so bad he's always getting people mixed up I shouldn't rely on him as a witness, but Quent's a good chap He and Wouter were great pals Your uncle Jem knows him, of course Sarah's uncle, I should say Max, would you do me a favour and go find out what's happening back there?'

'You don't mind being left alone with—'

'No '

Tolbathy's face was set hard, his eyes fixed on the tracks that had been so carefully ploughed clean of snow How was he going to feel about his precious toy from now on? This might be the last run he'd ever make Damn shame, Max thought, as he stepped back into the make-believe coal tender

There wasn't a great deal of extra space here, with the little stove needing its stack of firewood nearby and its zinc platform to keep it from setting fire to the wooden floor The coat rack was attached to the wall, as far away from the heat as possible, and the wraps it held had not been thrown down by the jolting stop, unless somebody had bothered to come and put them back. Max went over to have a look.

The hooks were jammed full of men's bulky overcoats, women's ancient minks, ratty beavers, voluminous capes of wool or velvet; plenty of things to hide behind if you needed to get out of sight in a hurry There was nobody here now Max went along the rack poking at every wrap to make sure.

Then he lifted the bubbling iron teakettle off the top of the stove and looked in. All he could see was a red-and-yellow shimmer, but that didn't mean somebody hadn't got rid of something here lately These airtight stoves burned awfully hot. There'd been plenty of time since the crash for anything flimsy, such as a false beard, to have been totally incinerated.

With some regret, Max peeled off his own dapper moustache and dropped it in to make sure. It flared up and vanished almost before it hit the coals  If there was anything to be found here, it would have to be sifted out of the ashes after the stove cooled down.

## CHAPTER 6

Max went on through to the parlour car, having to pass Quent Durward, who'd posted himself as watchdog in the vestibule as instructed. 'How's Wouter?' Durward asked, perhaps because he actually recognized Max or perhaps because he just assumed anybody coming from the engine would know.

'As well as can be expected,' Max told him, and kept moving  They'd all know the truth soon enough  Right now, from his impression of the so recently elegant parlour car, he'd say each passenger had troubles enough of his own to contend with.

Those who weren't still looking dazed and nursing their own or some friend's injuries were making futile efforts to straighten out the general mess. Though the train's usual furnishings were bolted to the floor, a number of extra chairs and occasional tables had been brought in for the passengers' convenience. These of necessity were small, flimsy affairs and most of them had gone flying when the train stopped, carrying with them crystal, napkins, ashtrays, beaded handbags, gloves, fans, smelling bottles, lorgnettes, pince-nez, and monocles guests had been laying aside after they'd made their initial effects.

Among the debris was a shocking amount of broken glass. It was dangerous to have around, but apparently nothing could be done about it right now except to pick up the shards one by one. Such implements as brooms and dustpans,

Hester Tolbathy had to keep explaining, were brought down from the house when the train had to be cleaned and taken back there afterward. She was begging everyone not to bother, but that only spurred them to greater efforts, as always happens when a hostess is most desperate for people to quit milling around and give her a chance to cope.

One dowager, though, took a dim view of risking her petticoats among the slivers. 'Why aren't the servants taking care of this?' she demanded.

'The servants? Oh, you mean the caterers,' said the much-tried Hester Tolbathy. 'I suppose they feel it's not their job, which it really isn't  Besides, they must be having problems of their own. Heaven knows what's happened to all that food they were getting ready to set out for the buffet. Could somebody please go and see? I don't dare leave my patient '

She was sitting on the floor with Mr Wripp's head in her lap, doling brandy into him from the end of a teaspoon. He looked worse than Wouter Tolbathy.

'I'll go,' said Max. He'd have gone anyway  Being so much the youngest and nimblest, he was in the caboose before anybody else could get started. There, he found three women in the trim black and white uniforms he'd seen earlier  As he'd expected, they were trying to reassemble the makings for what must have been planned as a truly sumptuous Edwardian supper. When they saw him open the door, one of the women giggled, somewhat hysterically.

'You'd better not come in here. We're picking your dinner off the floor. For Pete's sake, don't tell anybody I said that  Would you know if we're supposed to go ahead and serve, or what?'

'I'd say or what,' Max told her. 'It's an awful mess out there. We're headed back to our starting point, and should arrive any minute now. There are two serious injuries that I know of, I don't know how many minor ones, and the dining car's full of broken glass. What I expect Mrs Tolbathy will want you to do is take whatever of the food is salvageable to the house and set up your buffet there, so the passengers can eat quickly and get along home. Nobody's in the party mood any more '

'What a shame,' said the woman who appeared to be in charge of the catering crew 'It started out as such an elegant affair Pam and Angie and I were looking forward to serving the buffet. Mostly we get run-of-the-mill jobs like corporation luncheons and wedding receptions. What happened to the train, do you know?'

'Mr Tolbathy thinks it may have been a deer on the track,' said Max. That was as good a prevarication as any. 'By the way, where's your boss? The man with the fancy corkscrew?'

The woman called Angie shrugged. 'Marge was asking me that just before the train stopped. We thought he'd be back to see about the wines for dinner He's got nothing to do with us, though. He just breezed in here and started giving orders. Then he went off somewhere and we haven't seen him since.'

'When did you first see him?'

'Not long after we got started. We were getting the tray ready to serve the caviar We'd known that was supposed to be the opening number, as you might say. Mrs Tolbathy—she's a lovely woman, isn't she—she'd explained to us already what she wanted done. She'd got the chopped onion and sieved egg yolk and all that ready, or I expect her cook had, and brought them down to the train in plastic containers, along with the can of caviar. She even brought a can opener, in case we didn't have one with us. There was no reason why we couldn't have gone ahead and served it ourselves.'

'But then this man with the big chain around his neck breezed in and said he'd take care of it,' said Pam.

'Did he tell you who he was?' Max asked her.

'Nope. We naturally assumed he must be the Tolbathys' butler, so we stepped aside and let him do it.'

'What exactly did he do?'

'Nothing much, really. We'd set out the dishes that fit the

epergne, as I said, and started filling them, so he told us to go ahead and finish that part. But when I reached for the caviar, to open the can, he stopped me. There's this special glass dish, see, that had a place scooped out to fit it in the swan's back. I thought Mrs Tolbathy was taking an awful chance, myself, using that lovely epergne on a train ride Did it get damaged?'

'I couldn't say,' Max replied. 'So anyway, what did this man say?'

'He said that wasn't the way Mrs Tolbathy wanted it done. He told me just to put the dish and the can and the opener on the tray. He'd carry it out himself and open the can at the serving table to prove the caviar was fresh We'd never heard of such a thing before. Can you tell me what's so classy about hauling out a can opener in front of company?'

'Sorry,' said Max. 'I'm not much up on caviar, myself. Mrs Tolbathy didn't try to stop him when he did it and nobody else fainted or anything, so I suppose it was okay. But is that all this man did, just opened the caviar and vanished?'

'Well, he'd fussed about the champagne a little. We had it chilling in a tubful of snow and he sort of snorted at that. But Marge told him it was Mrs Tolbathy's idea—her tub, too, as a matter of fact—so he didn't say any more.'

'He wasn't with us more than a few minutes,' Marge amplified. 'We assumed that if he was supposed to be the wine steward, he'd be concerned about how we were handling the dinner wines, but he never even looked at them. See, here they are. Luckily we had the white wines chilling in the tub when the train stopped, and Pam managed to grab most of the burgundy, thank God. Everything got shaken up, of course, but we couldn't help that.'

'Our real tragedy was the turkey mousse,' said Angie. 'It's all over the walls and everything and would you believe we can't even find a sponge to wipe it up with? Somebody'll have to come out here tomorrow with a scrubbing brush and a bucket of suds. And it had come out so beautifully, too When I think of the hours we spent getting ready for this party, I could cry.'

'I'm sure nobody's going to blame you ladies for what happened,' said Max.

'That's not the point,' Marge told him. 'We take pride in our work. It hurts to see everything we slaved to get perfect messed around like this. Besides,' she admitted, 'we were hoping to make such a great impression that we'd be asked to do more parties for this crowd. Oh, well, that's life, I guess Would you please tell Mrs Tolbathy we're getting squared away here? We could be ready to start serving as soon as we get back to the house, if she can round up somebody to help us carry the food off the train.'

'I'll be glad to. Thanks a lot.' It wasn't Max's place to thank them, he supposed, but a kind word never hurt. They did seem to be taking that turkey mousse dreadfully to heart.

The train was slowing down now. They must be coming up to the tiny station. Hester Tolbathy was looking a degree less frantic when Max brought her the relatively good news from the caboose.

'You're quite right in telling them we'll be serving up at the house. I wouldn't dare offer food among all this broken glass, and one can't send one's guests away hungry. Though I must say, as far as I myself am concerned, I don't even want to think about eating. I hadn't realized train wrecks were so disturbing to the stomach.'

'Nor had I,' said a friend who'd been standing nearby, 'since you've brought it up. Oh dear, I wish I hadn't said that.'

The woman wadded a handkerchief over her mouth and dashed off towards the cloakroom. Hester Tolbathy began looking frantic again.

'I do hope Edith isn't coming down with something. Perhaps it's just the shock. Did he say how soon they could begin serving?'

'He who?' Max asked her. 'There are just the three women out there.'

'But what happened to the man who's in charge? The one who served the caviar so beautifully?'

'Hester, those caterers don't even know who that man was. They thought he was your butler.'

'Whatever for? Who has a butler these days? We certainly don't, just Rollo who does the yard, and we wouldn't have him if he weren't married to our cook Rollo's about eighty years old and smells like a goat. But if that man wearing the chain isn't one of the caterers, who on earth is he? And what's happened to him? Did you see him in the dining car, by any chance?'

'I haven't seen him anywhere, not since his performance with the caviar. And you haven't either. Right?'

Hester Tolbathy stared at Max for a moment, then shook her head. 'No, I'm sure I haven't. He got the caviar and champagne started, I remember, then went off I suppose I assumed he'd gone back to the caboose to start organizing the buffet. It didn't seem to matter. The caterers came well recommended and obviously knew their business, so I simply left them to it and concentrated on my guests. But how odd about that man with the chain. Who on earth do you suppose he was?'

'I've been hoping you could tell me.'

'But I can't. I'm quite positive I'd never seen him before, and I flatter myself I have a fairly good memory for faces. What a pity your Uncle Jem couldn't have been here. He knows absolutely everybody, and he never mixes up the names and faces. Oh, we're stopping. Thank heaven for that!'

## CHAPTER 7

They'd been on the train less than two hours altogether, but it felt like infinity Nobody was standing on ceremony about getting off. Men were fetching wraps by the armload and parcelling them out like handbills. A couple appointed themselves emergency conductors, got the doors open and the steps down Max remembered he was supposed to be escorting Marcia Whet and looked around for her She was, he saw, already bundled into her pelisse and boa, carrying her muff and the now absurd cartwheel hat in her hand Obed Ogham was with her, astonishingly sober and silent for one who'd acted so drunk and boisterous a little while ago

The pair of them stopped beside Hester Tolbathy. 'Hester, isn't there something we can do?' Marcia asked

'Yes, go straight to the house and phone for the police ambulance. Obed, get hold of that bartender and take him along with you. Show him where to set up and start him serving drinks. Tell Jessie to make hot coffee and send Rollo down with the handcart we use for the cleaning supplies. The caterers can load it with some of their stuff and let him push it back Tell Rollo to hurry And for goodness' sake, Marcia, tell that ambulance to hurry, too I don't like Mr Wripp's colour one bit.'

'I never did,' said Ogham with a flash of his customary charm. 'Don't fret, Hester. Wripp will live to bury us all Go ahead, Marcia. I'll catch up with you. How's the booze level up at the house, Hester? Should I take an armload of bottles from the bar here?'

'It wouldn't hurt, I suppose, if they aren't all smashed. Never mind about glasses. We have thousands. Oh, and tell the caterers they can get ready to move the food as soon as the cart comes. Thank you, Obed.'

A competent woman, Max thought. They'd need more than one ambulance, but she didn't know that yet. He knew he ought to go up and talk to the police himself, but he wanted to stick with the train a while longer There were things that ought to be found out before the cars got messed around worse than they were already.

His most pressing curiosity, of course, was about that man who'd opened the caviar If he wasn't a caterer or an employee of the Tolbathys', then who was he and where had he got to?

He could have jumped off when the train stopped back there in the woods, Max supposed. If that was the case there'd be plenty of footprints to follow, even though Tom Tolbathy claimed not to have noticed any. The snow was deep and unbroken everywhere, except along the ploughed tracks. He could have walked the railroad ties, provided he was fast enough on his feet to outrun the train, but what would have been the point? They didn't go anywhere except back here.

He might have got himself lifted off in a helicopter, or lassoed a tree limb and swung off Tarzan-fashion The thought of that correct, spruce figure wearing the Great Chain of the Convivial Codfish as he hurtled through the treetops was perhaps a trifle outré. Max was inclined to rule out snowmobiles and dogsleds, too

The train must have made at least one full circuit of the loop before that speedup and sudden stop, come to think of it They'd been travelling at an easy pace but hardly a crawl. Max could check that out with Tom Tolbathy later. The point was, he supposed, that the bogus sommelier could have jumped off right here at the station. That way he wouldn't have made noticeable tracks, but it meant he'd have been gone before Wouter was killed

But what could possibly be the point in his coming aboard just to put on that elaborate show with the caviar? Furthermore, how could he have left a moving train without attracting notice?

Two of the three caterers had been in the dining car by the time the sommelier disappeared; one of them making canapes, the other passing them around. Where was the third? If she'd also left the caboose, the man might have opened the outer door and jumped off from there.

It sounded easy enough, but was it? Max knew train doors were supposed to be kept latched and barred while the train was in motion for reasons of safety. Getting one of those heavy doors open against the drag of the moving train might not be easy, and jumping out of it certainly wouldn't be safe You might land in a cushiony snowbank, but you might also slide down and be crushed under the train

Assuming you made it safely, how would you close the door after you? Would the momentum cause it to slam and catch, or would the door stay open and call attention to the fact that you'd gone?

Any chance of escape from the dining or parlour car could be ruled out because there'd have been too many people around to grab you and stop you from doing something so crazy. The so-called coal tender didn't have any outside door, just the doors at the ends that led into the engine cab and the parlour car. Your best way out would have to be through the window of the cab, after you'd murdered the engineer. But why do that? You didn't slaughter a Comrade of the Convivial Codfish just to keep him from knowing you'd dressed up as a wine steward and played a practical joke on his brother's guests.

You might if you were the kind who went around greasing other Comrades' stairways How could that prankster have got hold of the Great Chain if he hadn't stolen it off Jem's neck at the meeting, or been given it by someone who had? How had anybody managed to steal the chain, if it came to that?'

The method wasn't Max's main concern right now. The point was, if you ruled out that one waitress at the Scrooge Day luncheon, as Jem was so sure you had to, then only some member of that insane chowder society could possibly have made off with the ponderous bauble. Being no doubt one of the Tolbathys' usual crowd, he'd have been invited to the party here and he'd have known about Hester's ritual with the caviar.

It would have been simple enough for him to trick the caterers into thinking he had a right to take over the serving, simple to do his little act, which consisted mainly of opening two bottles of champagne and one tin of caviar with a few fancy gestures thrown in for effect. And it would have been simplest of all to fake his escape by just taking off the chain, stashing it somewhere out of sight, and blending back in with the other guests.

But how would he have unblended in the first place? These false beards and walrus moustaches the men were sporting hadn't really fooled anybody, at least not for long. To begin with, they were too obviously fake. In the second place, the self-appointed sommelier hadn't been wearing any.

He'd sported natty sideburns, though, and a full head of greyish blond hair that might well have been a wig. His light blue eyes—Max noticed such things—had been somewhat prominent So had his teeth. His height and build had been average, his face more round than long, his age perhaps fifty-five, which would have been remarkably young for a Comrade of the Convivial Codfish.

On the other hand, it wouldn't have been too difficult in this flattering light for a Comrade to knock ten or fifteen years off his age with a wig to hide his bald spot and plumpers in his cheeks to smooth out the wrinkles. If he had false teeth, he could have put in a different plate. His grandmother's, for instance. A real old Yankee never threw anything away that might possibly come in handy sometime, and nothing changed a person's expression more than an ill-fitting set of dentures. If he wore glasses as a rule, he could have left them off, assuming he saw well enough without them to dish up the caviar and pour out a few glasses of champagne He'd managed that all right, Max remembered. He'd also worn clean white cotton gloves, either to dress up his act or because hands were often recognizable and fingerprints always identifiable.

As to his clothes, one elderly dinner suit looked so much like another that he'd have had no need to change. He wouldn't have needed to disguise his voice because in fact he hadn't uttered a word, except to the caterers, who wouldn't have known him anyway. All he'd need to do after he'd put on his brief performance would have been to step into one of the toilets, take off his wig, his sideburns, his gloves, and presumably his teeth, and resume whatever guise he'd come in as a guest He could have stuffed the Great Chain under his shirt, strolled back to collect his champagne and caviar, sauntered on through to the parlour car and thence to the tender, dropped his false hair, the gloves, and maybe even the teeth into the stove, stashed the Great Chain somewhere or other, and gone on to kill Wouter

It was a lovely plan, really In the confusion after the jolting stop, he could have rejoined the party and pretended to be as shaken up as the rest. They were all in such a state by then that nobody would have noticed. As to the Great Chain's turning up later on, that wouldn't matter so long as he hadn't left any fingerprints on it. Whoever found it would be intended to think some Comrade had planned a joke on Jem Kelling and abandoned the chain when he realized Jem was not among those present and that circumstances didn't lend themselves to slapstick humour

All right, so the missing wine steward was most likely the killer, most likely a Comrade, and most likely still at the party, if such it could still be called But which one of them was he? Max stood watching the passengers depart, trying to choose one who could have enacted the role of the steward.

The hell of it was, he had too many choices Nondescript, fairish colouring, average height, and unremarkable noses were the rule rather than the exception, as he'd noticed in

Jem's photographs earlier. There were a few antiquated Prince Alberts, but most of the men were wearing plain, old-fashioned dinner jackets and plain, old-fashioned boiled shirts Most still had on their false whiskers, determined to get their money's worth out of them even though the gaiety was to all intents and purposes over. Just about any one of them, according to Tom Tolbathy, could have known how to take over the train, speed up and stop short, creating enough confusion to cover his own shenanigans

Hester Tolbathy was still ministering to old Wripp, looking around with anxious impatience, doubtless wondering where her husband had got to Tom, poor devil, must be thinking about Wouter. Max went over and glanced into the tender Tolbathy was there, helping with the wraps, making sure none of the guests tried to get up to the cab

They'd have to be told fairly soon about Wouter's death, but it would be far better to put off the news until they'd been herded up to the house and the police had arrived Max went back and spoke to Hester Tolbathy

'Your husband's getting people off the train Why don't you go on up to the house with the others? I'll stay with Mr Wripp until the ambulance comes. They'll be along any minute, I expect.'

'Oh, thank you, Max. You're being terribly helpful.'

'Used to be a Boy Scout I'll just run in first and see how they're making out with the food.'

He gave Hester a smile of reassurance and went back to the caboose Marge, Pam, and Angie were still there, putting plastic wrap over bowls and platters and handing them out to an old man with a handcart, who must be Rollo.

'You haven't seen any more of that guy who was supposed to be helping you?' he asked Marge.

'No, and we've been trying to figure out where he went. We can't find him at all.'

'Maybe he climbed up on the roof of the train, like in the old Western movies,' Pam suggested.

'In a soup-and-fish, on a night like this? He'd freeze his corkscrew off,' scoffed Angie

'He didn't have a topcoat?' Max asked.

'If he had, he didn't leave it here. Those are ours, over there ' Angie pointed to a heap of bright-coloured down jackets thrown over a bench  There were no other wraps in sight.

'Would there be any place here in the caboose where he could have ducked out of your sight, even for a minute or so?'

'Sure, there's a washroom right next to the door into the vestibule.'

'Passengers will please refrain,' Pam giggled.

Max went over and took a look  The washroom was tiny, with barely room for a miniature sink and the kind of contained water closet common on planes and trains, but it would have served perfectly for a quick change. The door even opened backward into the caboose, so it would have screened his coming and going, and there was a mirror over the sink to help him get his face on straight. He couldn't have had a more convenient setup, as he'd no doubt known in advance.

'If you want my opinion,' Max told the three women, 'your wine steward was one of the guests, playing a joke on the rest of the party. I'm curious to know who it was. You can help me, if you will.'

'Sure,' said Marge. 'What should we do?'

'Just keep your eyes peeled up at the house. See if you can spot anybody who reminds you at all of the man you saw: looks like him, talks like him, uses a similar gesture, has any resemblance, however slight  If you do, point him out to me. If I'm not around, try to find out his name.'

'Finding him should be a cinch,' said Pam. 'He'll be the only one around without a moustache  I've never seen so many fuzzy faces since the hippies grew up and learned to shave.'

'It's all fake, you half-wit,' said Angie 'They stuck them

on for the party That man we saw must have taken his off to serve, then put it back on again, which is why we can't find him now '

'He'd have had to do better than that,' Marge pointed out sensibly, 'or his friends would have recognized him right away. Come on, we'd better get moving. You take the galantine of chicken, Angie Pam, can you manage the *coulibiac en croûte*? Mr Whoever-you-are, I don't suppose we could coax you into carrying this big bowl of salad for us?'

'Marge, that's unprofessional,' Pam chided

'So what? We can't spend half the night trekking back and forth Those people must be starving by now '

'Right,' said Max 'I've got to stick around and wait for the ambulance, myself, but I'll try to find you some extra hands.'

There were still a few stragglers getting off the train Max asked the less battered ones if they'd mind helping the caterers, left them to it, checked on the ancient Wripp, who appeared to be sleeping off all those spoonfuls of brandy now, and went into the coal tender.

Tom Tolbathy was still there, slumped on a bench beside the all-but-empty coat rack He looked utterly worn out but managed to raise his head when Max came in

'What's happening, Max?'

'The situation's under control, more or less They've moved the bartender up to the house and the caterers are getting ready to serve supper there. Your wife's gone along to start things rolling, and she's asked Marcia Whet to call a police ambulance for Mr Wripp.

'What about Wouter? Doesn't she know?'

'I didn't tell her. I figured she had enough to contend with already '

'God, yes! Poor Hester, she was so keen on this party So was I. We must have been out of our minds. Is anyone badly hurt other than John Wripp?'

'None that I could see. A few sprains and bruises and a

number of superficial cuts from broken glass. There's plenty of that around.'

'I can well imagine  How's Hester bearing up?'

'She's a terrific woman, Tom  How are you doing?'

Tolbathy grimaced 'As well as can be expected, I suppose. Max, about—what happened to Wouter. There's no chance you might be wrong?'

'How am I supposed to answer that? Nobody's infallible. All I can say is, if I'd thought there was a chance I could be wrong, I'd have kept my mouth shut in the first place Believe me, Tom, I don't go around yelling murder for the fun of it  You may be interested to know I've questioned the caterers about that guy who served the caviar wearing your Great Chain. They haven't the faintest idea who he was and they haven't seen him since he did his act  They assumed he must be your butler  Your wife tells me you don't have one.'

'Of course we don't. We live very simply, really  My mother had a butler, naturally, but we've just old Rollo, who prefers to think of himself as the caretaker  Rollo's not a bad old curmudgeon, in his way  Wouter and he were always great pals  He's going to be—where in blazes is that ambulance?'

'I don't suppose it's been ten minutes since they got the call,' Max reminded the importer.

So little time for so much to have happened. Max had experienced this queer stretching-out of time far too often before. Was Sarah back from the boarding-house yet? What was she doing around the apartment? Missing him, he hoped.

'Tom? Hey, Tom! What the hell's going on here? Where's Wouter?'

That was Obed Ogham, barging into the coal tender. From the state of his trouser legs, he must have slogged back to the train through the snow instead of sticking to the shovelled path. There was an expression on his florid face that Max couldn't interpret.

'Wouter's forward in the cab,' Tom Tolbathy told Ogham quite truthfully 'Do you have any news about that ambulance, Obed?'

'They said they'd be right along I put in the call myself.'

'Go give them another ring to ginger them up, will you, like a good fellow? How are things going at the house?'

'Not well at all.' Ogham sounded rather pleased to be the bringer of bad news 'People are reacting strangely to that fake train wreck Wouter pulled. You know, Tom, it wasn't really funny Fanny Dork's lost her bridgework down the loo, and Ed Ashbroom's sick as a dog. His wife's even sicker, but she's making less fuss about it. You know Ed Anyway, everyone's complaining of bellyaches and burning sensations in their throats and fighting to get to the bathrooms If you want the truth, I don't feel any too—'

Ogham proved his case by dashing out of the tender and off the train. When Max and Tom got to him, he was doubled over, clutching at his stomach, retching into a snowbank.

Tom Tolbathy stared down at the unlovely spectacle, his own face the colour of the snow. 'Good God, what's happening?'

'A combination of shock and too much to drink,' Max suggested 'You know how these things happen. One person gets hysterical and sets the rest off '

Max was lying and he knew it A less hysterical crew than this, he'd seldom run into There'd been no panic after the train stopped, only a sprinkling of high-toned expletives and a few indignant, 'Well, really's.'

As for drinking, by Bittersohn's own family standards most of them had indeed drunk a great deal and eaten shockingly little These were Jeremy Kelling's cronies, though, and judging from what he knew of Jem, Max realized they'd hardly begun Added to that, bellies trained on baked beans and boiled dinners didn't heave easily So far, Max had seen various of his new in-laws and their friends amorous, bellicose, and somose but almost never nauseated, except perhaps by a misquoted passage from John Greenleaf Whittier or a laudatory reference to Franklin Delano Roosevelt.

'Hadn't we better do something for him?' Tom was asking nervously.

'He'll be okay,' said Max.

After another heave or two, Ogham wiped his face with a handful of snow, then began mopping at himself with his handkerchief

'Don't know what's the matter with me,' he muttered 'You'd better have a sharp word with your liquor dealer, Tom, or quit making your own bathtub gin.'

Max studied Ogham's face in the light from the train. He was still flushed and his pale blue eyes were bloodshot, but he didn't look to be in desperate shape He certainly wasn't drunk in the usual sense of the word.

Taken simply as a face, Ogham's was not remarkable Now, with its customary arrogant expression wiped off, it could have been mistaken easily enough for one of the other men's. That was interesting. Max hadn't thought to include him among the possibles before, but he was in fact about the right build and type to have masqueraded as the vanished wine steward The question was, could he have subordinated that obnoxiously overbearing personality to a servant's role?

He wouldn't have had to keep it up for long Furthermore, what about the personality of the actor? If the man had been one of the Comrades of the Convivial Codfish, as his possession of the Great Chain appeared to indicate, he must have had the gall of an ox to risk pulling off his act in front of his closest friends Ogham qualified on that score, anyway Whether Ogham could have managed Wouter Tolbathy's murder remained to be seen, but Max personally couldn't think of anybody in this crowd he's rather hang it on.

'Obed, you'd better go back to the house and lie down a while,' said Tolbathy.

'Think I will.' Ogham was about two-thirds of the way

up the slope when a police ambulance screeched into the drive

'I'd better go to meet them,' Tom remarked with obvious relief. 'Will you stay here with Wouter, Max? And John Wripp, of course.'

'You might as well stay, too. They're coming down to the train.'

Ogham was waving and shouting, 'This way ' Men were coming to meet him, carrying a stretcher. He turned and led them toward the train but seemed to be having some trouble walking The ambulance men edged past him, until he was bringing up the rear.

'Understand you've got a problem here, Mr Tolbathy,' the man who was now the leader called out.

'Rather a serious one, I'm afraid,' Tolbathy replied with his eyes on Ogham. 'Obed, why don't you let one of these officers help you up to the house? Perhaps Hester can give you something to settle your—Obed, what's wrong? Catch him, one of you!'

Ogham was down on his knees in the path, clawing at his throat, grunting with pain

'Mac, you and Willy get him on to the stretcher, quick,' the leader ordered. 'Take him up and radio the hospital for instructions. Willy, you stay with him. Mac, bring the other stretcher. I understand there's a man with a broken leg aboard, Mr Tolbathy?'

'We're not sure, but he seems very ill. This way, please.'

Wripp was barely conscious now, the age spots standing out stark and brown against his tight-stretched yellow skin in pitiful contrast to the opulent crimson velvet pillow and lap robe Hester Tolbathy had used to make him comfortable The head of the ambulance crew knelt on the floor beside him and shook his own head

'He's in shock  Looks like we're going to need some help here. As soon as Mac gets here, could you two gentlemen slide the stretcher under him while we lift? If that hip's really broken, we don't dare juggle him around any more than we have to.'

'Of course,' said Tolbathy. He sounded relieved at the prospect of being able to do something. When Mac puffed up with the stretcher, Tom knelt at the old man's head, Max at the feet.

'Say when.'

Working together, the men got Wripp on the stretcher wrapped in a grey blanket, then passed straps around him to hold him safely in place.

'Can't take any chances with a man his age. It's kind of slippery on that path,' said the crew leader. 'Okay, that should do it. So that's the story, eh, Mr Tolbathy?'

'Well, no, I'm afraid it isn't My brother's dead up ahead in the cab You'd better send another ambulance'

# CHAPTER 8

They were going to need a whole flock of ambulances Somebody up at the house must have already pushed the panic button, for two more vehicles came hooting and flashing up the drive while Max and Tom Tolbathy were still at the train, waiting for the police cruiser the first crew had promised to send.

'Max, could you for God's sake go and see what's happening?' Tolbathy begged 'I know I ought to go myself, but damn it, I've got to stay with Wouter. Tell Hester. She'll understand. Besides,' his face twisted and he clutched at his stomach the way Ogham had done, 'I'm not sure I could make it'

'Jesus,' said Max, and went.

What the flaming hell was going on here? When he ran up to the mansion on the hill, he found the three caterers and an elderly couple who must be Jessie and Rollo the only ones really able to function. Hester Tolbathy was doing her gallant best, but Max could see she was in no better shape than some of her guests

'I don't know what's the matter with everybody,' she was groaning. 'Where's Tom? Is he all right?'

Max avoided telling her. 'Tom's still at the train. He sent me to say he'd be along soon They've got Mr Wripp away in the ambulance, you'll be glad to know.'

'And Wouter?'

Max had a bit of luck dodging that one, too Somebody who must be the family doctor was hurrying over to Mrs Tolbathy, looking frazzled and furious.

'For God's sake, Hester, what did you give these people to eat?'

'We'd only got to the caviar. Why, Fred? What's the matter?'

'I don't want to say for sure until we've had a chance to run the proper tests, but they're all showing symptoms of acute arsenical poisoning '

'Arsenic? How could they possibly? Oh, my God! Excuse me.'

Clapping a hand tight over her mouth, Hester Tolbathy darted away The doctor moved to go after her, but Max grabbed his sleeve.

'Just a second, please, doctor Tom Tolbathy sent me up to get a report on what's going on here Why do you say arsenical poisoning?'

'I didn't say that's what it is. I said that's what it looks like Vomiting, diarrhoea, burning sensations in the throat and skin, extreme weakness—those are typical symptoms. How do you yourself feel, by the way?'

'Fine,' Max told him.

'But you're a member of the party? You ate what the others did?'

'No, I didn't All I had was one small Scotch and water Most of the rest had champagne and caviar, but I don't happen to care for either.'

'What about those three waitresses or whatever they are? The women in the black uniforms. Did they have any?'

'I shouldn't think so.'

Max described the ritual around the epergne The doctor grabbed Marge, who was rushing past with a pile of clean towels.

'Just a moment. Did you eat any caviar?'

'What?' Marge blinked, then shook her head 'Oh, I get you No, I didn't have any and I'm sure neither of my helpers did It was opened and served right in front of the guests, you see '

'So I understand Was anything else served at the same time?'

'Just bread and melba toast and the usual garnishes Sweet butter, chopped onion, and egg yolk '

'Did you prepare these garnishes?'

'No, Mrs Tolbathy brought them to the train all ready to serve, except for putting them into the dishes '

'Could they have been tampered with on the train?'

'I don't see how. They were in plastic bowls with tight-fitting lids and we didn't open them until we were ready to take them in. We three were working right there in the caboose where the bowls were. Nobody else came in except the bartender. He picked up the olives and sliced lime and stuff for the bar, but he never went near the food.'

'Olives and limes don't count as food?'

'Not specially, in this case. Anyway, we had them ready on a separate tray at the far end of the counter, so all he had to do was pick them up and go out. I doubt if much of the stuff got used, but you could ask him.'

'I will. And who served the garnishes for the caviar?'

'I did. That is, I transferred them from the plastic bowls to the dishes that fit on the epergne. A man dressed up as a wine steward came and carried them into the dining car.'

'Did you watch him serve them there?'

'I didn't myself, but my two helpers did. Actually he didn't serve them, he only put the dishes on the epergne. Then he opened the caviar and went away. One of my helpers made the canapes, and the other passed them around to the guests. Doctor, you're not trying to say one of us three tampered with those garnishes?'

'No. I'm trying to pinpoint the probable cause of this outbreak because I'll have to make a report to the police and I want to get my facts straight. I'm correct in assuming, am I not, that not everybody would want the same garnish on his caviar? Some would want egg yolk, some onion?'

'That's right And once the girls had begun serving, people would come over to the table and fix their own the way they wanted it. You know how they do.'

'Yes, of course. But everyone took caviar in one form or another?'

'I should think so Who'd want a crackerful of plain egg yolk? Anyway, the dish was empty when we went to clean up '

'There were no leftovers at all?'

'Just some of the bread and butter and a few pieces of melba toast I'm sure of that because I washed the serving dishes myself Angela brought them out empty and I gave them a quick scrub because we planned to use the epergne again on the dessert table Fresh fruits, mints, salted nuts, chocolates—'

'Yes, yes And the empty tin?'

'I washed that, too It's a rule we have, always rinse out the empties On account of rats, you know Wasn't I supposed to?'

'You couldn't have known,' the doctor reassured her 'You didn't happen to notice anything wrong with the tin? A bulged top, anything of that sort?'

'Do you think I'd have been dumb enough to let it be served if I had?'

'But you did have a chance to look it over before it was opened?'

'Plenty of chances. Mrs Tolbathy brought down the can along with the garnishes. I saw it and so did my helpers. So did everybody on the train, if it comes to that, because the wine steward held it up for them to see before he opened it '

'He opened the caviar in the presence of the guests?'

'That's right.'

'Um. That clinches it, I believe. All right, thank you. I must get back to my patients. God knows how many more I've got by now. At least this explains why some are so much sicker than others Depends on how much they ate, I suppose. Damn Russians! If they can't get at us one way, they'll try another '

Max hadn't thought of that angle. He didn't think much of it now. Another fleet of ambulances came up the drive. He left the stretcher-bearers and paramedics to attend to those who'd been so merry such a short time ago, and went back to the train.

He might have known a crowd would have gathered. Naturally that procession of howling ambulances had attracted attention, notably from the news media. Several policemen who might otherwise have been making themselves useful up here were having, he found out later, to stay down on the road keeping the driveway clear so that victims could be got to the hospital Max cursed as he all but fell over a photographer with a camera perched on his shoulder and a young woman whose face he recognized from the evening news broadcasts They were arguing with a uniformed policeman who was guarding the steps into the parlour car.

'But we're from Channel Three.'

'I don't care if you're straight from the Garden of Eden,' the policeman told them. 'I've got orders to let nobody on the train Nobody means you, too, Mister,' he added for Max's benefit

'I'm a member of the party,' Max told him 'Mr Tolbathy's expecting me. He sent me to the house with a message for his wife, and he's waiting for an answer.'

'That's what they all say '

'Where is he, damn it? Tell him Max Bittersohn wants to come aboard.'

'Mr Tolbathy's talking to the chief '

'Good. I want to talk to the chief, too.' Max took out his wallet and showed his private investigator's licence.

The policeman shook his head 'That don't look like you.'

'My wife says I take a lousy picture Oh.' Max had forgotten about his side-whiskers. He reached up and pulled them off 'That help any?'

'Not much. You got stickum on your face '

'Come on, we're wasting valuable time. I've got some important information for the chief.'

'Yeah? About what?'

'I can't talk about it here '

The reporters were beginning to pester Max with questions He turned to glare That was a mistake because several photographers immediately took his picture, stickum and all.

'Come on, for Christ's sake,' he begged the policeman

'Just a minute '

The officer turned his back and said something to somebody inside. He must have got the right answer, for he squeezed aside and let Max go aboard.

The parlour car looked like the aftermath of a barroom brawl. Tom Tolbathy stood amid the shards, talking with a man in a more stylish uniform, who must be the local chief of police When he caught sight of Max, he stared as if he couldn't recall who it was. Then he blinked and nodded.

'Oh, Max What's going on up there? How's Hester?'

This was no time to be tactful. 'She's running her legs off. Your guests are all sick and there's a doctor who's talking about arsenic in the caviar.'

'Arsenic? That's absurd. And why the caviar?'

'Because I didn't eat any and I'm not sick, for one thing. Neither did the caterers, and they're okay, too. What about yourself? You said before I left that you weren't feeling well.'

'I'm not,' Tolbathy admitted 'Not really ill, but queasy.'

'Did you eat the caviar?'

'A bite of Hester's, that's all My God, is Hester poisoned too?'

'She was still on her feet when I saw her last.' Max didn't want to tell Tom where those feet were probably heading.

'What's this?' the police chief interrupted 'Where did that caviar come from?'

'There can't be anything wrong with it,' Tolbathy insisted 'It was the best Beluga, packed to my personal specifications, imported by my own firm, from a source we've been doing business with ever since my grandfather was alive. The tin was opened in front of me and all my guests There's no way it could have been tampered with '

'After it left the cannery, you mean '

'Why, yes, I suppose I do. But surely,' Tolbathy shook his head, 'that's unthinkable '

'Is it? Do you read the newspapers, Mr Tolbathy? Watch the news on television?'

'Yes, of course, but—'

'It's happened right here in our own country, hasn't it? Crazy people putting cyanide in medicine capsules before they're sold, poisoning jars of pickles on grocery store shelves. What makes you think all the nuts in the world are in America? Would there be any of this caviar left?'

'I doubt it,' Tolbathy replied. 'There never is. My guests know I give them the best.'

'Uh-huh. What about the can it came out of?'

'I expect you'll find that among the trash in the caboose,' Max told him. 'I doubt if it will help you any, though. One of the caterers says she washed it.'

'Washed it? What for?'

'It's one of their rules, she claims. So the garbage won't draw rats. It makes sense to me, Chief. My wife does it, too. You know how women are about rats.'

The chief said he did know how women were about rats. 'Where's your wife now? Is she sick, too?'

'She wasn't invited to the party. Actually, I wasn't either. I only filled in for her uncle, who was kept away. That's what I really wanted to talk to you about '

Max told his story. The police chief wasn't convinced.

'Seems to me you're trying to make something out of nothing, if you don't mind me saying so, Mr Bittersohn. I don't mean nothing, exactly, but the way I see it, we've got two entirely separate and unrelated circumstances here From the way you describe this club your uncle and Mr Tolbathy belong to, it's just a bunch of guys who get together now and then for a little harmless fun. Right, Mr Tolbathy?'

'Essentially that's pretty much the idea,' Tom agreed.

'Well, naturally a bunch of men like that, they play a few practical jokes on each other now and then. But what you're trying to tell me is that it's all one big plot First your uncle falls and breaks his hip because somebody's put wax on a flight of stairs he never uses and then calls up to tell him his false whiskers are ready I can see one of his buddies making a fake phone call to kid him about the whiskers, but the rest of it sounds pretty farfetched to me '

The chief appeared pleased with his own line of reasoning. 'As I see it, the janitor just took a notion to spruce up the hallway a little. Or maybe the landlord got after him to do it. So he threw some wax on the stairs to give them a little shine, make them look nice, you know He didn't bother doing too great a job because he knew nobody was going to use the stairs anyway You said yourself everybody takes the elevator except those two maids on the third floor, and they have to go down the back way, so they don't count.'

'But Jeremy Kelling's manservant questioned the janitor, and he claims he never touched the stairs '

'What would you expect him to say? He's not going to get himself in trouble for causing an accident. Would you?'

'I wouldn't lie out of it if I had '

'Well, individuals who empty trash cans for a living aren't likely to be so high-minded. Would you say so, Mr Tolbathy?'

Mr Tolbathy wouldn't go so far as to say so because he had little acquaintance among individuals who emptied trash cans for a living. He was willing to admit the hypothesis because he could see perfectly well, as who couldn't, that the chief was helpfully working his way around to suggesting Wouter Tolbathy's death might after all have been an accident, too.

Max could understand why. Tolbathy had a trainful of guests being carted off in ambulances because he'd allegedly served them poisoned caviar imported by his own firm. He was in trouble enough without a murder in the engine cab to top it off. Police chiefs in affluent suburbs didn't keep their jobs by being tactless over the problems of prominent citizens.

'But what about this vanishing man who served the poisoned caviar wearing the silver chain that was stolen from around Mr Kelling's neck at the club luncheon?' he protested.

Instead of answering Max, the chief turned again to Tom Tolbathy 'Mr Tolbathy, you're a member of this organization I expect you've seen the chain a great many times.'

'Oh, yes, and worn it, too I was the last person to hold the office Jeremy Kelling now occupies.'

'Did you yourself recognize the chain this man was wearing tonight as the one that was allegedly stolen from Mr Kelling?'

'No, I can't honestly say I did. The Great Chain has a big silver codfish about six inches long attached to it, you see. As I recall, this fellow was wearing a corkscrew on his chain That would have been enough to put me off, I expect. I'm not particularly observant about that sort of thing '

The chief nodded 'You weren't the only member of the organization at the party, were you?'

'Far from it. My brother was a member, though I suppose we can't count him. But there were several others: Ogham, Dork, Durward, Billingsgate, Ashbroom, Wripp—I can have my wife show you the guest list, if you like.'

'I don't think that will be necessary. What I'm getting at, Mr Tolbathy, is that none of these other members appeared to recognize the chain, either. Is that correct?'

'If they did, they didn't say anything about it to me.'

'Now, getting back to you, Mr Bittersohn. You yourself are not a member of the club, right?'

'That's right, but—'

'You've never been a guest at any of their meetings?'

'Guests are never invited,' Tolbathy answered for him. 'A silly rule, no doubt, but that's the way it's always been.'

'And you don't ever parade in public or anything? Like the Shriners, for instance?'

'Good God, no!'

'Then would you mind telling me, Mr Bittersohn, how you were able to make such a positive identification when none of the club members could? Where have you seen this chain before?'

'In photographs that showed my wife's uncle wearing it '

'I see.'

Case dismissed. Chief Whatsis was not going to give a damn that Max Bittersohn was an internationally recognized expert on silver chains and similar accoutrements. Chief Whatsis was going to shove the problem of Wouter Tolbathy's sudden, violent death under the rug and make damned sure it stayed there.

The hell he was.

## CHAPTER 9

'Where would you like to be dropped, Mr Bittersohn?'

That was Marge asking She and her helpers were taking
the untasted food and the unwanted investigator away in the
catering van. Tom Tolbathy, even as he himself was succumbing to an agony of stomach cramps, had made it plain
there'd be nothing more for any of them to do on his estate
He'd apologized very nicely, all things considered

Under the circumstances, Max could hardly have done
anything but leave, though he was inwardly furious at Tom's
insistence on a cover-up Besides, he didn't know where to
go

'I don't know,' he told Marge. 'Do you know of any place
where I could make a phone call, then wait for my wife to
drive out here and pick me up?'

'Sure, come on back to the shop with us. You can call from
there and have a bite of supper while you're waiting. We're
all starved.'

'Are you sure I won't be putting you out? Sarah will be
coming from Boston, and it may take her a while '

'That's okay We've got plenty to do at the shop. There's
all this food to cope with, for one thing. We can't just waste it.
Besides, since we got away from the Tolbathys' so much
earlier than we expected, we might as well put in the time
getting a few things done ahead. We don't often get the
chance to catch up, this time of year. But what a shame about
the Tolbathys' party. They're such lovely people.'

Max agreed the Tolbathys were lovely people and it was
indeed a shame. A damn sight worse shame than they
realized, but he wasn't going to tell them so. He leaned back
against the chilly plastic upholstery and marvelled at the sort
of mentality that would rather ignore a murder than make a

fuss, while the three caterers chatted about how best to recycle the sumptuous buffet they'd carted around all evening and never got a chance to serve.

Tolbathy was going to pay their bill in full, he'd told them, since it wasn't their fault they hadn't been able to do their job. Marge, Pam, and Angela were searching their souls as to whether they ought to take his money, even though they needed it to pay their suppliers 'What do you think, Mr Bittersohn?' Pam asked him finally.

'I think you'd be nuts to turn it down,' he replied. 'Knock off twenty percent if your consciences are going to bother you, and call it a goodwill gesture.'

'Great idea,' said Angela and went on lamenting the turkey mousse.

The catering shop was a cosy Victorian dollhouse done up in pink and white like a birthday cake 'It used to be the depot,' Marge told Max, 'till they took the local trains off We can't seem to get away from trains tonight, can we? Here, sit down, everybody. I'm going to pour us each a drink of that Jack Daniels we had for making the bourbon balls last week.'

'Good,' said Pam. 'I can use it. Angie, why don't you put the kettle on and I'll fix us a snack.'

She started filling plates with some of the more expendable delicacies. Max took a swig of his bourbon and dialled the apartment.

'Sarah? What's the matter? Good God, has it been on the news already? How did you happen to find out? Oh, Egbert phoned? Tickled pink Jem didn't get to go, I'll bet. Yes, it was apparently the caviar, and no, I doubt very much if it was the Russians. No, of course I'm not in the hospital. I'm in a catering shop surrounded by beautiful women trying to get me drunk.'

He drank some more of his whisky. 'Thanks, Marge, I owe you one. Look, sweetie pie, could you—no, not her You, for God's sake! Could you go get the car and come out here and pick me up, is what I was trying to say. How do I know where I am? Just a second '

Max handed the phone over to Marge. 'Would you mind telling my wife where to find me?'

Amused, Marge gave Sarah directions for tracking down her errant husband Then Max took back the telephone, admonished his wife to get young Porter-Smith or somebody to walk her down to the garage because there were too damn many weirdos around and he'd already had enough calamities for one night. Then he hung up and ate his supper

'My wife says they've been breaking into television programmes with special reports,' he told the caterers between bites 'The Tolbathys are going to love that Apparently some politician's already blethering about Communist plots to poison rich Americans and demanding a worldwide recall of Russian caviar '

'They can't do that,' wailed Pam 'Not over the holidays We already have six containers of caviar butter stashed away in the freezer '

'But that's not Russian caviar,' Angela reminded her. 'For caviar butter we use red caviar, which is just a fancy name for salmon eggs '

'I don't care. It's still caviar, and if we try to serve it everybody's going to start yelling we're a bunch of mass murderers Marge, I hate to waste the money we spent getting it ready, but we simply can't take the risk '

'Don't fret about the caviar butter, Pam,' Marge told her soberly despite the bourbon. 'What I'm worried about is how this is going to affect our entire operation.'

'What do you mean?' Angela protested. 'We didn't serve that caviar at the Tolbathys'.'

'We were there when somebody else did, and we didn't try to stop him. What do they call it? Guilt by association. You know what a flap people get into about poison in food. Not that I blame them. It's such an insidious thing. You can't see it; half the time you can't taste it. You don't even know you've swallowed it until you're—God, I hope all those people get better fast.'

Max decided not to pass on what Sarah had told him, that most of them were on the critical list and one other than Wouter Tolbathy was dead. The casualty was most likely to have been the old man Wripp, succumbing to shock and the injuries he'd suffered in falling; but that fact wasn't going to cut any ice with hostesses concerned about whether their own holiday revels were going to turn into nightmares like the Tolbathys'.

If he were in Marge's shoes, he'd be worrying, too. Damned shame. These were decent women and excellent cooks. He even took some of Angela's galantine of chicken, though he held stern personal views about the jellying of innocent poultry, and pretended he thought it was great because he didn't want to damage the caterers' morale any further than it was shaken already.

'As for business,' he mentioned, on the principle that misery might like company, 'if you think you've got problems, what about Tom Tolbathy? He not only stands to have his holiday profits and maybe his firm wiped out, he'll be lucky if his dear friends don't begin suing him for a million bucks apiece.'

'Oh my gosh,' said Marge 'I never thought of that '

'Maybe Tolbathy hasn't yet, either. But you can bet your pots and kettles somebody has '

As a matter of fact, Max hadn't thought of it either, until just now  He was still thinking when Sarah arrived in the beautiful car he allowed her to drive because he loved her even more than he loved his elegant conveyance, which was saying a lot. Besides, Sarah drove more expertly than most women, therefore infinitely better than most men

His wife was delighted to meet Max's new friends, accepted a cup of tea from Marge, salad from Pam, and a small helping of the galantine from Angela because it looked so delicious she couldn't pass it up  She talked cooking for a few minutes like a model guest, listened with the proper degree of horrified interest to the events of the evening, then bade the caterers a grateful farewell.

'I must get this poor man home. Thank you so much for taking such good care of him, and I do hope I'll have the pleasure of seeing you again. I'll drive, shall I, darling? You must be exhausted.'

Before Max could protest that he wasn't, Sarah was behind the wheel again. 'Where to next?'

'I thought we were going home '

'Not if you're planning to ditch the little woman and sneak back to the Tolbathys' by yourself That's what you have in mind, isn't it?'

'Sarah, two people are already dead '

'Three I heard it on the car radio coming out A Mrs Ashbroom is the latest. Did you meet her?'

'I suppose so. Her husband's one of Jem's buddies in that crazy goddamned chowder society, I know that '

'He would be! I hope Uncle Jem hasn't gone into a frenzy and discombobulated his hip. Max, this is awful Have you any idea how it could have happened?'

'Lots.' He gave her a brief rundown 'And a fat lot of good ideas are going to do me. What we need is evidence You take a left at the corner and keep going straight '

'Until we see the train, right?'

'You're a tantalizing wench, you know that?'

'I was afraid you were going to say a nagging wife Speaking of whom, I thought we might get your mother a tea cosy They have some lovely handmade ones over at the Women's Educational '

'Sounds terrific '

'What does?'

'Whatever you just said '

'She doesn't have one, does she?'

'So what if she does? Get her another '

'Max, are you sure you feel all right?'

'Sarah, you know I never eat caviar if I can help it. I only hope I survive that chicken. Why do women always have to go around jellying everything they can get their aspic on?'

'Why do some men feel compelled to be little gentlemen? Back there, you were acting as if that chicken was the most wonderful thing you ever tasted.'

'What was I going to do? Throw a tantrum and hurl it on the floor?'

'Must you always love or loathe? Can't you ever strike a happy medium?'

'You're suggesting I slug Cousin Theonia?'

'She's a palmist, not a medium  Furthermore, that remark was not amusing.'

'Your lips twitched.'

'How could you tell?'

'I have an intimate personal acquaintance with your lips, in case you'd forgotten.'

'You could be back home reminding me if you weren't such a workaholic. Has Mr Tolbathy asked you to take on his case?'

'Mr Tolbathy has told me ever so courteously to get lost.'

'I see.'

'The hell you do. I myself see those three nice chicken jelliers watching their nice little business go down the sink and Tolbathy losing everything he's got unless somebody does something pretty fast  The police won't  They're going to spare his feelings. Wouter Tolbathy's death is going to be an accident and the poisoning's going to be a nasty Russian plot. Tom Tolbathy's too sick to think straight tonight, but he'll be thinking plenty tomorrow when the Food and Drug Administration starts recalling his caviar '

'So you decided to do his thinking for him and bill him later  Crafty little dickens, aren't you?'

'I'm not the only crafty one around here. Damn it, Sarah, I wish you'd let me take you home '

'I don't see why. The murderer's not at the Tolbathys' any more'

'How can you be sure?'

'Elementary, my love. He or she is in the hospital. Isn't that where you'd be? You must be right about the poisoner's being one of the guests.'

'So how did he slip them the poison?'

'Maybe he does magic tricks and substituted a bad can for a good can in full view of the audience, like a bunny out of a hat. If he managed to get the chain off Uncle Jem's neck, he must be good at that sort of thing, wouldn't you say?'

'I hadn't thought of bunnies out of hats,' Max admitted 'So if he had the poison—'

'He'd give himself a tiny dose, make himself vomit as quickly and publicly as possible, complain a lot about burning sensations in his throat and whatnot, and get himself carted off in one of the ambulances with blaring of trumpets and beating of drums If the doctors couldn't find any trace of the poison in his stomach when he got there, he could tell them he'd been on a diet or something and only ate a weentsy nibble of the caviar to be polite.'

I only had a bite of my wife's. Tom Tolbathy had said that, and now he was getting pumped out with the rest of them. Good God, Max wondered, could Tom Tolbathy have engineered this gruesome farce himself?

Could he possibly have used his brother, Wouter, as the bogus wine steward, making Wouter believe it was only a joke they were playing on the guests? And then could Tom have killed Wouter so he wouldn't find out it wasn't a joke after all?

He could. In fact, Tom Tolbathy would have been in a better position than anybody else to manage the mechanics of such a plot He'd certainly have known what was planned with regard to serving the caviar, and so would Wouter They'd both been at the luncheon when Jem lost his chain;

mightn't one of them have pinched it while the other diverted Jem's attention by some trick?

'Another rabbit out of the hat,' Max finished gloomily. 'What I can't see is why the chain had to come into the picture at all. Unless it's because the server wasn't really one of the Comrades and the others were meant to think he was If that's the case, the plan fell flat. I seem to have been the only one in the crowd who recognized the chain for what it was, and I got called a liar for saying so.'

'Then maybe the Tolbathys just didn't want to go to the expense of buying a chain they'd never use again,' Sarah suggested.

'Sarah, you're talking about two guys who built their own private railroad for kicks '

'But they expected to get their money's worth out of the railroad '

Sarah was a bit puzzled as to why she even had to mention so obvious a fact  Cousin Dolph would have understood in a flash, and Dolph's was not the swiftest brain in the clan  So would Alexander, but she decided not to say so

Max shrugged  'If that makes sense to you, maybe it would to Tom Tolbathy  Okay, so let's suppose Wouter was the waiter  Has a nice ring to it, anyway  That means Tom would have had to be up in the cab running the train while Wouter did his act in the dining car. I can buy that. When I saw Wouter, he was wearing a striped engineer's coverall, but he could easily have swapped clothes with his brother They were close enough in size. Wouter'd have had plenty of time to put on the wig and do whatever he did to his face Tom could have done it for him, if it comes to that. Then Wouter could have dropped the wig and stuff into the stove on his way back to the cab '

'As for the chain,' Sarah cut in, 'Tom would have taken that from him and put it back around his own neck while they were changing clothes again. He'd have waited till they changed before killing Wouter, I should think, so he wouldn't have to bother about getting him back into his engineer's suit. Tom could have been wearing the chain under his clothes even while you were getting the horselaugh from that stooge of a police chief.'

'And Tom was so kindly not backing me up, saying he wasn't much good at noticing things like that. So where are we? Tom could have managed to spend five minutes or so in the engine without being missed. As host, he did a fair amount of backing and forthing. Anybody who happened to look for him and not see him around would naturally have assumed he was in another car. Even if someone happened to go up to the engine and catch Tom at the controls, it wouldn't matter. Tom could stick to the story that it was all a gag, postpone the execution to a more propitious time, and find some way to stop the guests from getting at the poison.'

'How, for instance?'

'Pull the train wreck ahead of schedule, maybe  Or stop the train, race into the dining car, and do a Marx Brothers routine with Wouter, snatching the caviar and running off with it or some damn thing. Since he's in the business, no doubt he had a few spare cans kicking around, so he'd just give Wouter an untainted one and make him go through the act again  I'm not saying it happened, I'm just saying it could have '

As to killing a beloved brother, how many persons of Max's usually brief acquaintance had deeply regretted what they saw as the necessity to bump off their nearest and dearest but gone ahead and done it anyway? Maybe Tom Tolbathy was as devastated about Wouter's death as he seemed to be  Strong men had wept often enough after they'd put down their favourite dogs or stabbed their mistresses

'Look at Don José,' Max said aloud

'Why? Where is he?' Sarah asked, naturally enough

'Oh, sorry  I was cogitating.'

'About Don José? You don't mean Carmen's Don José?'

'Whose else?'

'What would a love-struck tenor have to do with a trainful of people eating poisoned caviar?'

'To the best of my knowledge, nothing. How well do you know Tom Tolbathy?'

'I don't know him at all. To me, Tom Tolbathy is just another name on Uncle Jem's long list of drinking buddies. I think Alexander brought Aunt Caroline out here once to some benefit gala or other '

'He didn't belong to the Codfish crowd, did he?'

'Heavens, no. Alexander wasn't the fun and games sort You ought to know that by now.'

'How come we always get back to Alexander?'

'We don't. You're just in a snit because I won't let you play daddy the way he used to. I've had enough father figures in my life, thank you. Is this the Tolbathys' driveway? There's a locomotive painted on the mailbox. You still haven't told me why you said Don José '

'Sarah, dearest darling sweetie-pumpkin, I have no idea why I said Don José. I must have been talking in my sleep. Yes, this is the place Go on till you find a train, then stop '

## CHAPTER 10

'Max, I think I have to stop,' said Sarah

'Who says so?' Max mumbled with his eyes still shut.

'That policeman who's making the terrible faces at me.'

'Huh? Oh '

Max sat up straight, pushed the button that let down the window, and stuck his head out. 'Evening, officer. I'm expecting another official from the Food and Drug Administration. Has he arrived yet?'

'No ' The patrolman hesitated a moment, then added, 'Sir.'

'Blast it, what's keeping him? Mrs Bittersohn, didn't you

succeed in making Fothergill understand we have an emergency situation here? Never mind, officer, I quite understand it's not your fault. When he comes, will you please tell him I've gone on ahead. Where will I find Mr Tolbathy, do you know?'

'I think they took him to the hospital, Mr—'

'Then where's this man Rollo, the caretaker? At the train or in the house?'

'I wouldn't know, sir.'

'Well, I suppose I'll have to track him down for myself. You'd better stay here Not letting anyone up, I hope?'

Before the policeman could decide he wasn't letting them up, either, Sarah had gunned the motor and left him in the lurch 'So that's how you do it,' she remarked

'Sometimes,' Max admitted 'So Tolbathy's been carted off with the rest of them. Damn, I wonder if there's anybody left by now You wouldn't happen to know how to drive a train, *kätzele*?'

'One could always try '

'Let's hope we don't have to That's it, over there '

'Thank you for the information,' Sarah told him sweetly

'Now who's being snitty?'

'Well, dear, that train would be rather a hard thing to miss If you're planning to look for evidence, I'm afraid you've left it a bit late.'

A bent-over figure had just appeared at the open door of the parlour car and sloshed something from a dustpan into a large trash container that had been pulled up beside the steps Rollo, or someone, must be cleaning up

'I'm not,' said Max 'If there was any caviar left anywhere on the train, the police will have found it before they cleared out And if that silver chain's turned up, which I very much doubt, Rollo must surely have had sense enough not to throw it out. Let's go ask him Are you warm enough?'

He put an arm around Sarah just in case and caught up on some lost cuddling time under pretence of helping her over the path, now trodden into lumpy ice Rollo saw them coming and stood watching them from the doorway, casually propping his broom across the opening as a barrier

'Let me try this time,' Sarah murmured.

When they got to the steps, she looked up and smiled. 'Good evening. You must be Rollo I'm Jeremy Kelling's niece, Sarah. You know Uncle Jem, I'm sure.'

She was rewarded by a momentary flash of badly stained dentures. 'Busted 'is hip,' rasped the caretaker.

'That's right. He's still in the hospital, driving the nurses crazy as you can well imagine. This is my husband, Max, who was in the party tonight. May we come aboard?'

'I got orders not to let nobody on.'

'Those idiotic police, I suppose. Expecting one man to cope with a mess like this. Here, let me have that broom. Max, you go forward and see what needs to be done in the tender. Rollo, you'd better come down here and pick up this glass that's been spilled beside the trash barrel before somebody slips on it and gets cut. Mrs Tolbathy would have seventeen fits if she knew you were down here slaving away by yourself at this hour. How is she, have you heard?'

Somehow or other, Sarah had become a member of the family Rollo meekly did whatever she told him to while Max prowled. His search was not fruitful. After a while, he came back to where Sarah and Rollo were still sweeping up glass.

'No luck up there. Rollo, did the police find any trace of the poison?'

'Them?' Rollo snorted. 'They couldn't find their own—' he glanced at Sarah and decided perhaps he wouldn't finish that remark 'Hell, no, they ain't found nothin'. Ain't found out who killed Mr Wouter, neither. Accident, they're tryin' to call it. Accident, my backside! How's a man goin' to fall an' bust 'is Adam's apple when there ain't nothin' handy to bust it on, answer me that?'

'I pass,' said Max.

'Furthermore an' besides, Mr Wouter wouldn't never o'

been dumb enough to have an accident in the cab nohow. I ain't sayin' Mr Wouter didn't do some funny things now an' then, but what man hasn't? What the hell, if a man wants to dress up like a coot when he's goin' swimmin', why the hell shouldn't he? Might not make no sense if he'd dressed like a turkey cock, say, or one o' them roadrunners from the desert. But coots an' water, that's sensible enough if you look at it the way Mr Wouter looked at it. See, that was the thing about Mr Wouter '

Rollo was leaning up against the red damask wall by now, quite content to let Sarah push the broom while Max held the dustpan for her. 'Like I was sayin', Mr Wouter always made sense. His kind o' sense, anyways An' what don't make sense is for a man to go monkeyin' around with the throttle an' cause a God-awful mess like this here, then go an' get hisself kilt for no damn reason So what I tried to tell them damn flatfeet an' what I'm tellin' you now is, he never done it.'

'You're saying Wouter would have known better than to speed up and stop short, even if he meant it as a joke,' said Max.

'Joke, hell! You don't play jokes with a movin' train. Mr Wouter loved this here train like she was 'is sweetheart. Snuggled up to them controls same as you was doin' with the missus down there comin' over the path. I seen you an' you needn't think I didn't,' Rollo leered 'Old enough to know better.'

Rollo must have been mopping up the whisky as well as the debris, Max decided. He probably wasn't drunk, but he certainly wasn't sober. This might not be a bad time to suggest a train ride.

'I expect you know how to run the train as well as Wouter did,' he observed craftily. 'I wish I did. You wouldn't by any chance care to take my wife and me down the track a little way.'

'Dunno but what I might. Soon as we finish cleanin' up here.' Rollo was even less befuddled than Max had taken him to be, unfortunately. They had to stay on the dustpan detail another fifteen minutes or so before they got their ride.

And then it turned out to be a tedious waste of time  They chugged along at ten miles an hour through snow-covered woods that got awfully boring after a while. Max stood next to Rollo because he didn't trust the gleam in the old goat's eye, keeping Sarah well out of fumbling distance on the opposite side of the cab

'Look for footprints or other signs of disturbance in the snow,' Max had told her, but there were none to see Everything was smooth and sparkling as the seven-minute icing on one of Cousin Theonia's chocolate layer cakes, except for a tragic little patch where rabbit tracks suddenly came to a floundering stop. Sweeping traces of a great, feathered wing and a few small bloodstains showed Wouter Tolbathy's hadn't been the only violent death out here tonight. However, nowhere could they find any indication that the man with the chain had jumped off anywhere along the line  Max hadn't expected any, but he'd felt duty-bound to check before anybody came tramping alone the line and spoiled whatever signs there might have been.

So now there was nothing left to do but thank Rollo for the ride and go home. First, though, Max used the house phone in the tiny station to phone up to the house for the latest bulletin from the hospital.

'No more casualties, thank God,' he announced. 'But your wife, if that's who it was, sounds awfully upset about Mr Wripp.'

'Huh. Small wonder.'

With that maybe not so enigmatic remark, Rollo stumped off toward the house  Sarah and Max went back to their car.

'You don't suppose old Wripp lived up to his name?' Sarah murmured. 'I suppose he did grow up in an era when it was still considered dashing to seduce the housemaids, come to think of it  Any woman married to Rollo wouldn't mind getting seduced now and then, I shouldn't think.'

'You never can tell,' said Max. 'Maybe Rollo spends his spare time out in the gardener's shed with the lady next door.'

'If he does, she's no lady Miserable old wretch, making me slave over that broom half the night.'

'Poor *fischele* I'll drive this time. Why don't you shut your eyes and take a little nap? You could rest your head on my shoulder,' Max offered kindly

'Thank you, darling ' Sarah took advantage of the offer but knew she wouldn't be able to sleep. 'Did we accomplish anything at all, do you think?'

'We helped Rollo clean the train, anyway. And we've pretty much established the fact that the fake wine steward must have been one of the guests. I thought so all along, but it's never safe to take anything for granted. You hauled off a neat bit of gate-crashing there, by the way. We'll have to put you on the company payroll '

'That will be nice. What do we do next?'

'Next, we go home to bed '

'You do come up with lovely ideas. Sweetheart, are you sure about the tea cosy?'

'I'm sure about wanting to go to bed with you.'

'When were you ever not? But you're sweet to say so '

Sarah relaxed for a while in the warm darkness, enjoying the feel of his coat sleeve against her cheek 'I got your sister Miriam a really handsome porcelain soufflé dish,' she said after a while. Cousin Theonia's going to copy out her secret recipe for noncollapsible spinach soufflé to go with it.'

'Do I like spinach soufflé?'

'Who says you're going to get any? Besides, Miriam doesn't have to use the dish for soufflé if she doesn't want to.'

'What else would she use it for?'

'Miriam will think of something, never fear.'

Max's elder sister was almost a better cook than Cousin Theonia, though Max liked Sarah's cooking best of all because she was the only one who could fry eggs to suit him.

She was frying one the following morning when she remarked, 'I suppose I ought to go down to the hospital pretty soon. I think the Educational's going to be open this afternoon, and I did want to get over and buy that tea cosy for your mother before they're all gone.'

'Tell you what,' Max said with his mouth full of grapefruit. 'You get the cosy and I'll visit Jem.'

'Are you sure you feel up to it? He was in an absolutely dreadful mood yesterday '

'He can't scare me  Do I smuggle him in a hip flask of martinis, or what?'

'I'll make him an eggnog the way Aunt Appie used to make them for Uncle Lionel, half milk and egg and the other half brandy. He was fit to be tied yesterday because they hadn't put any gin in his orange juice. I can't decide whether Uncle Jem's an alcoholic or just a Regency buck born out of his time.'

'If you ask me, he's a mythical monster  When are you going to make the eggnog?'

'Right now '

Sarah poured milk into the new blender Max had bought her, broke in an egg, added milk and brandy, and pushed one of its fourteen buttons at random. She was the first of the Kelling tribe ever to own one and had an atavistic feeling that her grandmother's wire whisk would have done the job just as well, though she wouldn't for worlds have let Max know. One of the things she hadn't counted on when they got married was his penchant for coaxing her into the twentieth century while there was still enough of it left to make the experience worthwhile

Anyway, the blender did make a perfect eggnog, though Uncle Jem would have been equally content with an imperfect one so long as she hadn't stinted on the brandy  She added a little sugar and a grating of nutmeg and poured the foaming mixture into a plastic ice-cream carton her mother-in-law had sent her full of carrot tzimmes, in an attempt to bring civilization to Beacon Hill. The elder Mrs Bittersohn had been aghast to learn that neither Sarah nor any of her relatives had ever tasted tzimmes and, moreover, didn't even know what it was.

A thermos bottle would have made a less inelegant container, but Sarah knew Max would never remember to bring back the bottle. The only one she had was a valuable family heirloom her father had been wont to take with him on his mushrooming expeditions.

Cousin Mabel had always maintained Walter had kept the bottle full of ipecac in case he picked toadstools by mistake, but that was just Cousin Mabel and nobody had ever paid any attention to her, least of all Walter Kelling. He hadn't paid any vast amount of attention to his only child either, if it came to that. However, Sarah still had enough filial piety not to send his personal relic into that bourne whence no thermos returneth.

## CHAPTER 11

Max recoiled fastidiously from toting a recycled tzimmes container down Charles Street, but yielded willingly enough when Sarah put it into a little brown paper bag for him He then kissed his wife, as was his habit, and walked over to the hospital, where he found Jem Kelling propped up in bed raising hell.

'Hi, Jem,' he said. 'You're in good voice today, I see. Sarah sent you a pick-me-up.'

'Thank God there's still one woman in the world with an ounce of human compassion in her bowels,' he snarled.

'Don't bother glaring at me,' said the attendant nurse 'If I had any human compassion in my bowels, I wouldn't last long with patients like you. Speaking of which, did you void this morning?'

'What kind of question is that to ask a man in front of company? Of course I did. Think I'm a goddamn camel?'

'You mean camels don't?'

'How should I know? It's a figure of speech. Go away.'

The nurse went, promising to come back soon and visit further indignities upon him. Jeremy Kelling replied, 'Pah!' and got busy on his eggnog. Max Bittersohn watched until Jem showed signs of beginning to mellow, then opened a large manila envelope he'd brought with him and took out a group photo of the Comrades of the Convivial Codfish he'd extracted from Jem's album.

'What's that?' asked the Exalted Chowderhead. 'A get-well card the braw lads sent me? Bless their scoundrelly hearts. How was the party? Did you give everybody my heartiest greetings and fondest wishes for a rotten evening without me? Was nobody left standing when the fun was over? Who last beside his chair shall fa', he is king among us a', as the poet Burns so aptly put it. A jolly rout and revel it was, no doubt.'

'Rout,' Max told him. 'Not revel. I gather you haven't been listening to the news.'

'On that abominable squawk-box?'

Jem snarled at the television set that had been put before his bed in a misguided effort to cheer him up when he preferred to stay furious. Then he looked at Max and shadows crept back over the countenance that had so recently begun to brighten.

'What do you mean, a rout?'

'The only one left standing is myself, as far as I know,' said Max. 'The rest of the party got lugged off to the hospital.'

'For God's sake, why?'

'Suspected arsenic poisoning was the diagnosis when they started loading the ambulances. Here, I picked up a *Globe* on the way in.'

'Damn Democratic rag' Jem held the paper at arm's length and squinted. 'Great jumping Jehoshaphat! MURDER

ON THE OCCIDENT EXPRESS. SOCIALITES DOWNED BY POISONED
CAVIAR AS CHAMPAGNE FLOWS ON LUXURY TRAIN. THREE DEAD,
FIVE ON CRITICAL LIST.'

He read on, his eyes bugging. 'It doesn't say arsenic here.
It says—what the hell does it say?'

Max looked over his shoulder. 'Colchicine? That's a new
one on me.'

'Used in the treatment of gout,' said the nurse who'd come
back to shove a thermometer into Jem's mouth and take his
blood pressure. 'Isn't it weird about those people on the
train? You wouldn't happen to know any of them, I don't
suppose?'

Jem snatched the thermometer out. 'If I hadn't broken my
blasted hip, I'd have been on that train myself. So I sent this
incompetent knave instead,' he jerked the thermometer con-
temptuously at Max, 'and look what happened '

The nurse took the fragile glass rod away from him and
stuck it back under his tongue. 'That's nothing to what could
happen to you if you don't straighten out and fly right. You
ought to be counting yourself lucky you missed the party
Colchicine can be horrible stuff if you get too much of it.'

'Why?' Jem mumbled around the thermometer 'Wha'
happens?'

'Haemorrhagic gastroenteritis, intense weakness and ab-
dominal pain, respiratory failure, maybe a few other things.
If you survive, it might still raise the dickens with your
kidneys,' she added with that brisk, clinical detachment
laymen are supposed to find reassuring.

She picked up Jem's wrist and glanced at her own watch
'If they make it through the next day or so, I expect most of
them will be all right  There must have been an awful mess
on that train when they started feeling the effects. Boy, I'm
glad I didn't have to clean it up.'

The nurse dropped Jem's wrist, wrapped the blood-
pressure cuff around his arm, pumped it up, watched the
needle fall, shrugged, and jotted figures on Jem's chart. 'If

you were at the party,' she asked Max, 'how come you didn't get poisoned too?'

'Because I don't like caviar is the only thing I can think of I must have been the only person aboard who didn't eat any '

'A likely story Tell it to the judge.'

On that jocular note, the nurse took out the thermometer. 'What does it say?' Jem demanded.

'Normal, of course. So's your blood pressure I wouldn't dare measure my own, since I've started taking care of you Have a good day.'

She flashed them a smile and bustled off to inflict her brand of mercy on some other sufferer Max picked up the photograph again

'Okay, Jem Let's get to work.'

'Don't be ridiculous. I'm in no condition to work Damn it, how can you even mention that filthy word in my presence at a time like this? My oldest and dearest friends dropping around me like flies. I don't suppose Obed Ogham is listed among the demised?' Jem inquired, as one who seeks a candle to light the darkness

'Last I saw of Ogham, he was clawing at his belly and puking all over the Tolbathys' front lawn,' Max replied 'Does that make you feel any better?'

'Somewhat. Not wishing the revolting oaf any hard luck, mind you. I'm only thinking of his detrimental effect on the environment. What did he say about me last night?'

'Nothing, actually. He made rather a point of letting me know that for him the Kellings simply didn't exist. Look, Jem, how well do you know the Tolbathys?'

'Know them? Good gad, man, Wouter and I got expelled from Phillips Andover together That sort of thing establishes a spiritual bond, you know. Comrades, Comrades, ever since we were mewling infants. I assume I must have mewled. I'm sure Wouter did. How is the old buzzard, by the way?'

'I gather you haven't finished reading the paper,' said Max.

'What's that supposed to mean? Wouter's got a stomach lined with solid boiler plate. Damme, it would take more than a slug of gout medicine to fell Wouter.'

'It did I'm sorry, Jem, but that's how it is. Wouter got stopped in the engine cab with what looked to me like a karate chop across the windpipe. The police are calling it an accident, but you'll notice they're not trying to explain how the accident happened. Are there any ex-commandos among your Codfish crowd?'

'Commandos?' It took Jem a while to come back from the shock of hearing Wouter was dead. Then he sighed and shook his head as if to start his brain working again 'Oh, I get you. That hyoid bone thing. We all know about it. Ogham demonstrated the method at one of our meetings when he was feeling playful Ogham was a commando himself, or likes to pretend he was.'

'If he didn't do it himself, he must have given a damned effective demonstration. This was a fairly professional job, I'd say. Would anybody else in your crowd have had that kind of training?'

'I shouldn't be surprised,' said Jem. 'Most of us were in World War II. We've still got a few veterans of the previous encounter, if it comes to that. You say Wouter was at the controls when it happened?'

'He was, or had been. What happened was that we'd been going along at a nice, smooth pace. All of a sudden the train speeded up, then stopped short.'

'Sending everybody tip over teakettle, no doubt '

'Right. There were some fairly bad falls and a lot of broken glass. Tom Tolbathy and I went forward to see what had happened and found Wouter dead on the floor of the cab.'

'My God, what a blow for Tom. He and Wouter—I simply can't picture one without the other. It's like vermouth without the gin. Damn it, Max, if I ever get my hands on the bastard who scragged old Wouter—'

'You might be able to help me find him.'

'How?'

'Jem, Wouter's death wasn't the first peculiar thing that happened on the train To begin with, your silver chain showed up.'

'What? The Great Chain? Egad, where is it now?'

'I don't know The chain vanished again So did the man wearing it '

Max related the puzzling incident of the wine steward who did not exist 'So it looks to me,' he went on, 'as if the man had to be one of your Comrades, or else the accomplice of one Almost certainly, he was a bona fide guest at the party. That's why I brought this photo along. I can see several men in the group who are about the right size and general appearance to have carried off the disguise this guy was wearing. What I want from you is any information you can give me about who they are and what they do. That may possibly give some kind of starting point for an investigation. Are you game to try?'

'Of course Who's your first suspect?'

'Wouter Tolbathy.'

'Are you out of your mind? Wouter couldn't smash his own throat.'

'Who's saying he could? He might have acted the part of the wine steward, though.'

Max explained why he thought so. Jem heard him out, for a wonder, without interrupting Then he shook his head.

'I see what you're driving at, but I can't quite buy it. Mind you, I don't say Wouter wouldn't have impersonated a wine steward. What the hell, I'd have done it myself, if I'd happened to think of it and could see any fun in it, which I must say I can't. Furthermore, what do you mean by saying this bird had taken the Codfish off the Great Chain and hung a corkscrew in its place? That Codfish was welded on for all eternity, dammit '

'I'm sure it wasn't,' said Max. 'Most likely it was linked into the chain by a little silver ring Otherwise it would have hung stiffly and looked like hell I daresay anybody who had any skill at all with small tools could have made the substitution easily enough

Jeremy Kelling scowled 'Another illusion shot to hell. But what I actually started to say was, who'd be crazy enough to trust Wouter with a stunt like that?'

'You're saying Wouter wasn't reliable?'

'Oh, he was reliable enough, in his own way. That is to say, if Wouter said he'd do a thing, he'd do it. The problem was, you could never be sure how Wouter marched to a different drummer. For instance, if you asked him to serve that caviar, he'd have been more apt than not to come waddling in with a live sturgeon flapping around in a goldfish bowl I gather this bogus cork-snatcher didn't pull any fancy tricks?'

'The entire performance looked like a fancy trick to me,' Max replied. 'According to the caterers, however, it was Hester Tolbathy herself who laid on the epergne and the swan.'

'I'm sure she did. That's standard procedure at the Tolbathys' Hester inherited that epergne from her great-aunt and naturally she wants to get some good out of it. No sense in having a thing like that kicking around costing you a fortune in silver polish unless you make it earn its keep.'

'Sarah thinks that's essentially why one of your Comrades took the Great Chain instead of buying one of his own.'

'Nonsense The Great Chain's paid for itself long ago. The exalted Chowderhead wears it at every meeting, dammit.'

'Yes, but look at the other side of the coin. Sarah's argument was that this bird didn't want to go out and buy a new chain because he'd never get another chance to use it. She has a point there, you know. How often does a person disguise himself as a wine steward in order to bump off a trainload of people dressed up like Diamond Jim Brady and Lillian Russell?'

'I suppose it makes sense if you look at it from that angle,' Jem conceded. 'However, I wish to go on record as stating that I find the procedure contrary to the true spirit of conviviality and correct parliamentary procedure. Furthermore, I intend to propose a pretty damned stiff vote of censure at the next meeting.'

'Against whom?'

'Against the scurvy rotter who put my goddamn sacred insignia of office to such an ignoble purpose, that's whom. And you'd damn well better make him cough it up, Codfish and all, because I'm not pig-sticking that goddamn disgusting pink valentine without it, by gad!'

'Then we'd better get on with the job here. Your contention is that we can wash out Wouter Tolbathy on the grounds that nobody in his right mind would have involved Wouter in a conspiracy to murder, it being a foregone conclusion that Wouter would have loused up the plot one way or another. Right?'

Jem tried shifting his position, felt the pain, and cursed 'On sober second thought, much as I deplore the adjective, perhaps Wouter did louse it up. Wouter suffered from occasional attacks of gout.'

'Good God,' said Max. 'That's one I hadn't thought of. What you're suggesting, I presume, is that Wouter managed either by intent or by accident to dump his gout medicine into the caviar and that whoever put him up to serving it gave him a chop across the windpipe out of pique because he'd spoiled the joke. Is that it?'

'Makes sense, doesn't it?'

'Not a hell of a lot from where I'm standing If in fact Wouter had poisoned his brother's guests, the only sane course would have been to tell them so and serve out a round of ipecac.'

'Do you have to be disgusting? Blast it, I'm a sick man already.'

'You could be a damn sight sicker,' Max was unkind enough to remind him. 'Jem, hasn't it dawned on you yet that somebody tried to murder you, too?'

'What are you talking about?'

'That fall you took was no accident. Egbert and I found the proof. The reason you slipped on the stairs is that somebody had waxed the treads, shut off your electricity so that you wouldn't try to use the elevator, and put through a fake phone call alleged to be from Fuzzleys', knowing you'd go charging out of your flat like a wounded water buffalo and do precisely what you did.'

'But why?'

'Obviously, to keep you from attending the Tolbathys' party'

## CHAPTER 12

'Well, I'll be switched.'

Oddly enough, Jeremy Kelling appeared not only interested but downright flattered by what Max told him. 'Of course. What would you expect? Naturally no maniac in his right mind would dare start anything with me around.'

'So I was told.'

'You were?' Jem was looking downright perky by now 'By whom, for instance?'

'Your friend Marcia Whet, for one. She claims you have a fantastic ability to recognize anybody you've ever seen before, and that nobody could get away with any disguise if you were among those present'

'As a matter of fact, Marcia's perfectly right. I can spot 'em a mile away. It's just a knack You know, like Mozart dashing off *Cosi fan tutte* with one hand while he mixed a fresh batch of martinis with the other.'

'I'm not altogether sure Mozart drank martinis,' Max objected.

'And what if he didn't? You can be damned sure he drank something. Ever know a genius who was a teetotaller?'

'My acquaintance among geniuses is limited,' Max confessed. 'However, I understand your particular form of genius is common knowledge, among that crowd you hang out with.'

'Oh yes, they're always testing me one way and another. I've never missed so far.'

'Then wouldn't that be a logical motive to keep you away from the party? Whoever waxed those stairs apparently didn't give a damn whether you broke your hip or your skull, but was determined to disable you either temporarily or permanently If his object was to keep you from recognizing the Great Chain—which, by the way, nobody noticed but myself, as far as I can make out—his method strikes me as pretty damn drastic. Therefore, I'm operating on the premise that the chain was incidental, and that his impersonation was no joke but part of a premeditated mass murder plot. Do you follow me?'

'I'm a long way ahead of you Count me in on the action, my boy. Bearing in mind, needless to say, that it may be a while before I can take a step without that goddamn birdcage around me,' Jem scowled at the aluminium walker parked in the corner beside his bed,' and some nattering female at my elbow, no doubt. Try to describe this alleged wine steward, will you?'

'He was between five feet nine and five feet eleven inches tall, allowing for possible lifts in his shoes. Medium build, lightish complexion which was probably natural because I doubt if he'd have had time to fool around with makeup Age anywhere between fifty-five and sixty-five, maybe even older but not stooped or badly wrinkled Pale blue eyes, no glasses.

Light greyish-blond hair that was almost certainly a wig. Long matching sideburns which were also fake, no doubt. No moustache, mouth probably distorted by false teeth that didn't fit right. So we can assume he's clean-shaven, at least partially bald, wears dentures—'

'Bah. Call that a description? What about his clothes?'

'Ordinary black dinner jacket and pants, fairly well-worn, with satin lapels and satin stripe down the trouser legs. Ordinary mother-of-pearl studs and cufflinks. He was wearing gloves '

'What the hell for? What kind of gloves?'

'White ones, like Sarah's butler  So that nobody could get a look at his hands, which may have had some distinctive feature about them. So he wouldn't leave fingerprints. Because that's how he visualized himself in the role. Take your pick.'

'Canny devil. Could have been Dork. He always has a hangnail on his left index finger. I'd know Dork's hangnail anywhere '

'Does he know you would?'

'I don't suppose so. It's not the done thing to comment on another person's hangnail, you know. I learned that at Fessenden. Before they kicked me out, needless to say. What about the hairs in his nostrils? Did they curl up or stick out straight?'

'I'm afraid I didn't notice,' Max admitted. 'The light on the train was pretty dim.'

'H'm, this is going to be harder than I expected. Dash it, man, have you no eyes in that head of yours?'

'Jem, how many links are there in the Great Chain?'

'Links? What's that supposed to mean? How the hell should I know?'

'Can you tell me what's engaved on them?'

'*Honi soit qui mal y pense.*'

'The chain has twenty-two links, each formed from a solid silver plate approximately two inches deep by one and three-eighths inches wide, folded around oblate silver rings having an aperture of one-half inch, engraved with a deeply incised design of what looks to me like stylized rockweed and nicely gadrooned on the edges. The chain is a handsome piece of craftsmanship wasted on a pack of Yahoos, so don't give me hairs in the nostrils '

'You don't have to be offensive, dammit. *Chacun à son gout*, that's all.' Jem pronounced 'gout' as in colchicine, and appeared to be pleased with himself for having done so. 'Didn't you notice anything whatsoever about this foul miscreant except the colour of his eyes? Dash it, you've described about half the Comrades so far '

'I told you that was my problem before we started. Look, could we just run down the list? You tell me whatever you can about each of the possibles and I'll take it from there. What about Dork, since you've already mentioned him? Why's his hangnail on the left index finger instead of the right, for instance? Is he left-handed?'

'Good guess, my boy. You're wrong, of course. Dork's hangnail is on the left instead of the right because he's a gardener. He has a greenhouse roughly the size of Harvard Stadium in which he pots. What he does is to poke a hole in the potting soil with that left index finger and bung in a seedling with his right hand. Dashed monotonous performance to watch, I can tell you from sad experience. If you're planning to investigate Dork, you'd damn well better be on the *qui vive*. First thing you know, he'll have you backed into a corner and start telling you about his compost heap.'

'That's one of the hazards of my profession. What does Dork grow in this greenhouse of his?'

'Plants, I suppose. What else is a greenhouse good for?'

Max decided to skip that one. 'Does Dork do anything other than pot seedlings?'

'Writes books about plants. How to get closer to your cacti, that sort of thing. I don't suppose anybody ever reads them, but it doesn't much matter. Dork inherited half the family's fertilizer fortune, then married his third cousin and snaffled the other half. Dotty Dork's a gardener, too. He pots 'em, she plants 'em '

'Sounds like an ideal marriage Any homicidal mania in the family?'

Jeremy Kelling shrugged. 'Who knows? There generally is, isn't there? I've never seen any symptoms in Dork so far, if that's what you're getting at I suppose if he ever ran out of things to bury in his compost heap—sounds like a thin motive to me, but one never knows '

'One sure as hell doesn't,' Max agreed. 'Can you think of anything else I ought to know about Dork? Is he a railroad buff like the Tolbathys?'

'You might say so, in a tangential sort of way Dork acted as landscaping consultant when Tom and Wouter built their station, I know. Gardens around railroad stations are Dork's big thing. Whenever things slack off in the potting and planting department, Dork and Dotty hop over to Britain and ride around on all the little local trains They get off at every station and chat with the stationmaster, admiring his aphids and telling him what he ought to have growing instead of what he's already got, spreading sweetness and light generally. They used to do the same thing over here but these days there aren't enough stations left to bother with. Dork goes blethering around about the decline of art.'

'Dork wouldn't take umbrage and plot revenge if Tom and Wouter had happened to flout his advice and plant tulips instead of roses or whatever?'

'Confound it, Max, how am I supposed to answer that? I'd say it was damned unlikely. I also find it damned unlikely anybody would sneak around buttering my front steps in an attempt to effect my demise, but here I am, a shattered hulk with a stainless steel Ping-Pong ball in my backside. And there's poor old Wouter trying to play Fair Harvard on his brand-new harp with his halo on cockeyed and his wings upside down, like as not. And I don't suppose I'll even get to attend his funeral wearing the Great Chain as befits my rank and function.'

Jem was about ready to burst into tears. Max diverted him by pointing at the face next to Dork's 'What about this guy? He was on the train.'

'Ed Ashbroom? Good gad, didn't the paper say Ed was dead?'

'Not him, his wife '

'Oh?' Jeremy Kelling put on the most enigmatic expression his misleadingly cherubic facial contours would permit. 'How very interesting.'

'Why?'

'Max, you can't expect me to answer that To rat on a Comrade is the act of a cad '

'In other words, Ashbroom's been playing around '

'You said it I didn't.'

'Is the woman pressing him for marriage?'

'Dash it, how should I know? I don't slink around listening at keyholes.'

'Jem, for Christ's sake! This is one hell of a time to trot out your scruples. How serious is this affair of his?'

'I honestly can't tell you. All I know is that Ed and his wife have lived in a state of armed truce for years and Ed has been rumoured to seek consolation elsewhere. A number of elsewheres, I believe, but generally only one at a time. Ed's not one to stick his neck out beyond reasonable limits '

'Has there been any talk of a divorce?'

'Never, to my knowledge.'

'Why not?'

'Money, I suppose. That's what it usually boils down to, isn't it?'

'Which of them owned the pot?'

'I believe it was a case of jointly held assets. There was no family connection as with the Dorks, but Ed's and Edith's grandfathers were in business together. They got their finances so fantastically intertwined that after they died, their respective sons found it simpler just to go on with things as they were. That naturally made a bad matter worse. By the time everything trickled down to Ed and Edith, they decided it would be simpler to marry than attempt to sort out the confusion  Both of them resented having to do so, and each naturally held the other responsible for the fact that they couldn't get along '

'So now Ed gets to scoop the lot '

'Rather a coarse way of stating the position, but I expect that's what it will amount to '

'Does Ashbroom have any other source of income than his inheritance?'

'Don't be vulgar  Edward Ashbroom toileth not, neither doth he spin  He does, however, consider the lilies of the field  Ed's another gardener, like Dork '

'Why do you call Ashbroom Ed and Dork Dork?'

'Because Dork's first name happens to be Donald.'

'My God!'

'His parents couldn't have known at the time,' Jem apologized for them, 'but it's been a terrible cross to bear. Dork feels his affliction keenly  I understand his own sons won't even allow their children to have rubber ducks in their baths, for fear Grandpa might cut them out of his will '

'A hard man, eh?'

'Dork's been known to wax testy under provocation. As who hasn't, curse it '

Jem tried shifting his weight again, twisted his hip the wrong way, and uttered harsh words of wrath.

'Want me to crank up the bed for you?' Max offered

'Better not. That female Savonarola will only come galloping back here and crank it down again for the pleasure of watching me writhe in agony. I'm surprised she doesn't have a set of thumbscrews hitched to her stethoscope. Where were we?'

'Establishing the hypothesis that Comrade Ashbroom may not be altogether shattered at finding himself wifeless and in full control of their scrambled assets. You'd started to tell me about his gardening. What sort of gardening?'

'The usual sort, one would suppose. Ed plants things and they come up. Or not, as the case may be.'

'Where does he plant them?' Max could be a patient man when on a case, however tortuous the trail and weary the winding.

'In his garden, naturally Oh, I see what you're driving at. He's a neighbour of the Tolbathys' out in Bexhill Owns a paltry fifty acres or so. I expect that gives him room enough to cultivate the blushing rose and the chaste violet '

'No doubt Where does he park his passion flower while he's messing around with the chaste violet?'

'Not bad, my boy. Mind you, I don't know whether she is in fact a passion flower or just a clinging vine. She may be a Radcliffe graduate, for all I know I've met ladies of culture and refinement in the chorus at several of our more distinguished burly houses back in the dear, dead days beyond recall. Did I ever tell you about Mildred?'

'No, but if you think you're going to tell me now, forget it We have urgent business on hand, in case that small fact has slipped your memory. Getting back to the lady of culture and refinement, does she live in Bexhill, too?'

'Gad, man, you paint a yeasty picture of our suburbs Which no doubt doesn't half begin to do them justice It's my impression that Ed's current inamorata lives right here around the Hill somewhere, or possibly over in the Back Bay They've been seen together in the Copley Plaza and the Ritz bar. Rumour hath it she's red-haired, voluptuous, and about forty years younger than Ed, though as we both know, a lady's age is always open to interpretation. So are the imaginations of some of our Comrades, I must admit Not to mention their eyesight '

'Speaking of eyesight,' said Max, 'what about this man Durward? Is he as blind as he makes himself out to be?'

'How blind are you talking about?'

'Well, for starters, he mistook me for somebody named Ernest who used to sing madrigals with him.'

'Clumsy artifice. Quent Durward didn't mistake you for anybody. He no doubt heard you breathing and didn't smell face powder, so deduced you were present, alive, and probably not female; and took a shot in the dark, so to speak. His object was to make you talk on the chance he'd recognize your voice Quent's full of sly tricks. People put them down to his nearsightedness, little recking they're the guile of a conceited man who refuses to admit he's been legally blind since 1963. Quent's no doubt your murderer.'

'What makes you say that?'

'Logic, my lad, pure logic. It's always the most unlikely chap who did it. By some laughably simple ruse, once the modus operandi has been exposed. No doubt Quent had a seeing-eye dog concealed on the train somewhere and used it to lead him to the caviar A Russian wolfhound in this case, one would think.'

'Sounds reasonable to me,' Max conceded 'Can Russian wolfhounds be trained as railroad engineers?'

'Damn it, Max, use your head Guided by the smell of engine grease, Quent could have found the controls easily enough The dog would then have leaped out the window of the cab and run along the track in front of the train emitting woofs or bays or singing the 'Internationale,' or whatever Russian wolfhounds do, so that Quent could follow the sound '

'Damn, I hadn't thought of that But what happened to the dog after the train stopped?'

'Lolloped off to keep a rendezvous with a red setter bitch, or something of the sort. Don't bother me with trivia.'

'And what would have been Durward's motive for giving himself and the wolfhound all this trouble?'

'Good question I'll have to mull it over when this goddamn hip of mine quits giving me hell He'll have a sound reason, you may be sure of that. Quent's a shrewd thinker.'

'What does he do when he's not thinking?'

'About what any sensible man would do, I expect. Mixes himself a martini. Records tree toads.'

'Would you run through that last bit again, please?'

'I said records tree toads. What's so remarkable about that? Spring peepers, you know Those little creatures that hang around swamps at night making that infernal racket Quent goes out at night with a tape recorder and gets them to peep into his microphone. Then he plays you the tapes, unless you take stern measures to prevent him He claims he can tell what they're saying I can't think why he'd want to know, myself What in blazes would a tree toad have to talk about, anyway?'

Max could think of no reply except, 'Have we exhausted the tree toads?'

'It takes one hell of a lot to exhaust a tree toad, in my experience The ghastly things keep yammering away till all hours When one leaves off, another chimes in. All right, quit glaring at me like that Which of my bosom buddies do you want me to rip up the back next?'


# CHAPTER 13

'How about your friend Ogham?' Max suggested

'How, indeed? Now you're beginning to talk sense Since you're looking for double-dyed perfidy, there's one bastard who has it leaking out of him at every pore '

'What about guile?'

'Ogham?' Jeremy Kelling snorted 'Guile takes at least a smattering of intelligence.'

'Would you say that observation was based on fact or prejudice?'

'I suppose it's mostly prejudice,' Jem admitted 'If it was a question of thinking up some more rotten form of iniquity, I expect Ogham could be guileful enough '

'Why should he direct his iniquity against the Tolbathys? I thought he was a relative of theirs '

'Not Tom's, Hester's. Hester has a good bit of money in her own name, and Obed would like nothing better than an opportunity to exert undue influence. He'll never manage it so long as Tom's alive, because Tom's far too intelligent a man to trust that lout any farther than he could throw him. Which, *entre nous*, Tom would not be averse to doing.'

'Why doesn't he?'

'Because Hester entertains a warmhearted though chuckle-headed fondness for Obed He's the only son of her favourite aunt, or something of the sort. Tom is disgustingly uxorious, so he puts up with Obed for Hester's sake '

'Assuming both the Tolbathy brothers were out of the picture, would Ogham have any realistic hope of getting a chance at Hester's money?'

'Oh yes, I should expect so Hester had one of those old-school papas who thought it was unfeminine for a woman to show any head for business, and she still tends to think Papa knew best. Rather charming, I suppose, in these days of rampant feminism.'

'Rather dangerous, you mean,' Max grunted. 'Would she stand any chance whatever of not getting skinned by Ogham?'

'Not unless her children intervened, and she probably wouldn't let them know what was happening till it was too late. She'd feel she had to be loyal to Obed, even though he doesn't give a damn about her. In my highly biased opinion, Obed Ogham hasn't one scintilla of feeling for anybody except himself His mother spoiled him rotten when he was a brat, and he grew up thinking he was the pearl and the rest of the world his oyster. I straightened him out on that score back when we were at Rivers together '

'Before they expelled you?'

'Oddly enough, I never did get kicked out of Rivers. I can't think why not It wasn't a lax administration, by and large.

In any event, Obed's never had a decent word for me since that time, and the feeling couldn't be more mutual You didn't make the mistake of adopting a conciliatory manner last night, I trust?'

'I thought I'd made it plain that I never got a chance, assuming I'd had the inclination,' Max reassured him 'We never even got introduced.'

'Marcia Whet's doing, I expect Out of respect for me, she made sure you needn't be subjected to the ignominy of having to exchange civilities with that blight on the landscape Wonderful woman, Marcia. Good God, I hope she's going to be all right '

'So do I,' said Max, uneasily recalling the enthusiasm with which Mrs Whet had been wading into the caviar 'At least the paper didn't mention her among the casualties '

'That doesn't mean much,' Jem growled 'These morning editions go to press before midnight You wouldn't remember what it used to be like up on Newspaper Row, back when the *Globe* and the *Post* were still being published there. The presses would be clanking inside those big old wooden buildings and some young cub would be out on the sidewalk chalking up the latest bulletins on big blackboards. We'd stand around and read 'em off, then go down into Pi Alley and hoist a few with the newspapermen. Tom and Wouter and I And now Wouter's gone and Tom's in the chowder up to his eyeballs, and I'm lying here helpless. God damn it, Max, you've got to do something!'

'That's what I'm here for,' Max reminded Jem with considerable forbearance. 'What bothers me about Ogham is whether he could keep his fat mouth shut long enough to put on the act. The so-called wine steward didn't speak a word, except to the caterers out in the caboose, who wouldn't have recognized his voice '

'How long was he onstage, so to speak?'

'Not more than five minutes, I shouldn't think.'

'Five minutes isn't much. I expect Ogham could restrain

himself for that length of time in a disreputable enough cause. As for the acting, he could have managed that all right. Ogham's a lawyer, or used to be. No doubt he's been disbarred by now for some sordid reason or other, but I'm told he used to be noted for his courtroom histrionics '

'That doesn't surprise me He's the type. But how could he have got hold of the Great Chain? Since you and he have this running feud on, wouldn't he have had a pretty hard time stealing it from you?'

'I still can't figure out how anybody in the group could have stolen the chain. Since it did in fact happen, however, I'm forced to admit Ogham had as much of a chance as anybody else He was atrociously miscast as the Ghost of Christmas Present. That meant he had occasion to approach the chair a good deal oftener than suited me, I can tell you.'

'Who miscast him?'

'Comrade Billingsgate headed our Miscasting Committee this year.'

'Seems to me I met some Billingsgates on the train Which is he?'

'This one here, next to Wouter '

Max groaned. 'Jesus, another clone What the hell do you do, pick out a sample and then order them by the dozen?'

'The resemblance doubtless has something to do with the fact that they're all related, one way or another Billingsgate's a nephew of poor old John Wripp, who was connected somehow with Hester and Obed Bill's not a bad chap, except for an inclination towards good works. Around this time of year, he tends to break out in a rash of sweetness and light and hit us all up for donations to buy gifts for widows and orphans. I told him I've bought enough gifts for widows already. Did I ever tell you about Imogene?'

'Was she the one with the wreath of forget-me-nots tattooed around her hernia scar?'

'No, that was Isabelle. Ah, there was a woman!'

'Weren't they all? Is Billingsgate married?'

'Naturally, Bill believes it's better to marry than to burn, as Saint Paul so ungenerously put it. As a matter of fact, Bill's wife is Edith Ashbroom's second cousin  Or was, till now '

'My God.'

'Nice woman. Abigail's her name  She keeps bees '

'In her bonnet?'

'No, in beehives  Drat it, Max, this is no time for facetiae  Abigail grows fields full of heather or daisies or some damn thing, then turns the bees loose among the flowers  They go buzzing around with pollen all over their backsides collecting the honey, then Abigail brews the honey into mead  Great stuff, mead  Ever try it? Blows the back of your head right off. She sells it to some outfit that runs mediaeval orgies '

'Enterprising of Abigail  Is this bootleg mead, or does she have a meading licence?'

'Oh, I expect Abigail meads on the up-and-up  Bill's too high-minded to let his wife get involved in anything illegal  I wouldn't have been averse to a spot of mead-running myself, when I was younger and fleeter of foot  I wouldn't mind attending one of those orgies, either, only I don't suppose there's really anything orgiastic about them  Somebody hands you a chicken leg to chew on and lets you throw the bone on the floor is about what it amounts to, I expect. What fun is there in that?'

'It could depend on who's behind you when you heave the bone. How come Billingsgate supports spurious orgies in the first place, if he's so damned high-minded?'

'He calls them cultural experiences, no doubt  Furthermore, Bill doesn't support them, they support him. Anyway, they support the bees  They use the mead money to pay the taxes on the clover fields.'

'I thought you said heather.'

'Maybe I did  I fail to see that the point is worth arguing. What the hell does a bee know about botany, anyway?'

'More than you do, I'll bet. Getting back to Billingsgate,

what does he do when he's not peddling mead to the orgiasts? Run the still or talk to the bees?'

'As a matter of fact, Bill owns a string of overwhelmingly genteel radio stations They broadcast poetry readings, organ music, improving lectures, that sort of thing. Bill goes on the air and pontificates now and then.'

'Fun for him, no doubt; but it doesn't sound like a fast way to get rich '

'Oh well, there's the advertising for the mediaeval orgies and whatnot I expect they pick up the odd dollar that way On the whole, Bill does fairly well for himself. He mentioned at the meeting that he'd bought Abigail another Rolls-Royce as a Christmas present '

'To chase the bees in?'

'No, I expect she'll just stick it in the carriage house with the rest of them.'

'What rest of them? How many Rolls-Royces do they own, for God's sake?'

'Six or eight Old ones, naturally. Bill wouldn't be so vulgar as to own a *new* Rolls They drive them in auto shows Bill maintains antique cars are a sound investment.'

'He's right, if you can afford to tie up your money that way. Does Billingsgate know how to drive trains as well as Rolls-Royces?'

'I'm sure he knows how to operate Tom Tolbathy's, if that's what you're getting at He also fools around with model trains. Can't see it myself. When I fool around, I prefer to have the object of my foolery do a little fooling back.'

Jem was tottering on the brink of another reminiscence. Max took stern measures.

'Jem, I'm not interested in your lubricious past. Keep your mind on the calamitous present, can't you? What about this man at the end of the row?'

'Oh, him. That's Gerry Whet. You can wash him out. He's still in Nairobi.'

'You're sure of that, are you? What's he doing there?'

'Buying something or other. Diamonds, manganese, tiger skins. Who knows?'

'If it's tiger skins, the game warden knows and he's most likely in jail by now.'

'Wait a minute,' cried Jem, 'I remember. It's pyrethrum. Stuff they put in bug juice. Comes from some revolting pink daisy. Marcia had a corsage of the damned things at the farewell party she threw for Gerry before he left. She claimed he'd bought it for her to wear while he's gone because her chastity belt's worn out. Awful stink to the flowers I'll bet she wasn't wearing them on the train.'

'She was wearing a lot of other stuff, but I don't recall any pink daisies. What does Whet do with the pyrethrum after he's bought it?'

'I told you, kills bugs Gerry manufactures farm and garden sprays. You know, stuff they put on the cabbages to keep the butterflies from chomping on the leaves Gerry's been getting concerned about polluting the environment, so he experiments with natural plant poisons Pyrethrum's one of the old standbys, I believe, but he also messes around the greenhouse with pots of monkshood and ratsbane, muttering incantations to the gibbous moon, according to Marcia. Gerry gets a kick out of that stuff Can't say I feel any urge to try it, myself.'

'Considering the present circumstances, it's as well you don't go in for hatching exotic poisons Damn lucky for Whet he's still in Nairobi, if in fact he is. When's he due back?'

'After he's finished picking the daisies, I presume. Before Christmas, I'm sure Gerry and Marcia always make a great to-do over the holidays. Grandkiddies gambolling around the Christmas tree, stockings all hung by the chimney with care, the usual nonsense. I suppose you and Sarah will—or won't you?'

'We're doing a triple-header. Sarah's cooking up something with my sister Miriam for Chanukah, something else with Brooks and Theonia for Christmas, and God knows what with Mary and Dolph for New Year's. As I understand it, Dolph's borrowing Cousin Frederick's 1937 Marmon and we're all supposed to pile into it and drive over to Anora Protheroe's and listen to George's bear story.'

'Good God! Break a hip, my boy. It's the only way.'

'Don't kid yourself. The latest addition to the festivities is a homecoming bash for you, so save your strength while you can. Don't tell me they're serving lunch already?' Max added as food odours wafted into the room and dishes began clanking in the corridor.

'Speaking of poisonous substances,' Jem began gloomily, but Max cut him short.

'I've got to get this show on the road. Give me a few addresses, will you?'

He scribbled quickly in the little black notebook he always carried, then dashed out, leaving Jem to face creamed chipped beef on toast and no martini to wash it down.


## CHAPTER 14

Max wasn't sure the addresses were going to help him any The people he wanted to see were probably still in the hospital or possibly on their way to the morgue As for calling to find out, he might as well quit before he started The hospital switchboard would either be swamped with calls or shut down. There'd be police at the doors to keep anybody but their next of kin from reaching the patients in so sensational a mass poisoning. Rather than chase wild geese all the way to Bexhill, he might as well go after the ones nearer to hand first.

Tracking down Edward Ashbroom's pied-à-terre seemed to be as good an exercise in futility as any. It wasn't listed in the phone book, but Max hadn't expected it to be. Jem had thought the place was on Joy Street somewhere. He hadn't known the number, but Joy wasn't a long street. Max didn't suppose. Ashbroom himself would be there, but he hoped the girlfriend might He smiled a little to himself, recalling those daughters of joy who'd given the street its name back in the wicked old days before dating bars. Ashbroom must be a traditionalist

How many stiff-collared legislators had slipped out the back doors of the State House for a spot of innocent merriment between vetoing bills for civic betterment and voting themselves pay raises in years gone by? Of course nothing of that sort happened nowadays, with a governor who preferred the subway to a state limousine and whose idea of a bacchanalian revel was to send out for a corned beef sandwich with free pickle on the side. All honour to his name, Max thought, and might his constituency never grow less, sending his silent orison in the general direction of the gilded Bulfinch dome that once dominated Boston's skyline and now looks so puny against all that glass and concrete.

He was walking up Cambridge Street musing on the horrendous events of the previous evening, trying to sort out the calls he had to make to certain of his connections in various places on sundry continents, and wishing he'd stayed in bed an hour or so longer, when something caught his eye It was, actually, a speck of dust from the sidewalk kicked up by the foot of a man walking briskly ahead of him. Max took out his handkerchief, pulled at his eyelashes the way they'd taught him in Boy Scouts to free the eyelid, and blinked to dislodge the offending particle.

By the time he'd got his eyeball rid of its encumbrance, the man was well ahead of him, just another dark overcoat in the offing. It did seem, however, that there was something familiar about the way he walked. Recalling Jem's lecture about hairs in the nostrils, Max stepped up his own pace.

He was a fast walker at any time When he put on a spurt, he could outpace most joggers. It wasn't long before he overhauled the other man.

'I beg your—'

That was as far as he got. A Salvation Army lassie and her collecting pot had been beside him on the sidewalk. Somehow, all of a sudden, Max was entangled with her, her cauldron, and her tambourine. Be it said to the credit of that dedicated band that as they were sorting themselves out, the lassie was almost as solicitous for Max's well-being as she was for her scattered quarters and dimes.

'Bless you, sir Are you hurt?'

'Bless you, too,' Max answered politely as they helped each other to their respective feet and set the tripod upright 'No, I'm not hurt. Are you?'

'Not enough to count towards martyrdom,' she answered cheerfully, pulling her navy blue cape with its red trimming straight over her many layers of winter clothing. This was in truth no lassie but a middle-aged woman, her face reddened by exposure on many street corners at many Christmastides, her smile grown tolerant as such people's smiles must do lest they fade altogether. Max smiled back as he gallantly retrieved her tambourine for her

'Did you happen to get a good look at that man who shoved me into your kettle?' he asked her.

'Is that what happened?' She gave the tambourine an experimental rattle to make sure it still worked. 'I wondered how you came to stumble, because you have such a sure way of walking No, I'm afraid I didn't notice him particularly I was more interested in you, wondering why you were chasing him.'

'Was it that obvious?'

'It wouldn't have been to most people, I don't suppose, but I guess I'm what you'd call a trained observer Out here on the streets, you know, we have to be on the lookout for any strayed soul who starts acting funny Much as we want to believe the best of everybody, we have to deal with them the way they are, not the way we'd like them to be That's why we put wire over the tops of the kettles,' she added, poking down a dollar bill that was trying to get away

Max took the hint and fished in his pocket for change 'I

was chasing him because I thought I recognized an acquaintance.'

'If you say so, brother  It's none of my business '

'If he's who I think he is, I met him out in Bexhill last night, on a train. Would that jog your memory a little?'

'You're police, eh? I'm not surprised. I figured that story about the Russians was a lot of baloney.'

She thought a moment, then shook her bonnet and raised her heavily padded shoulders in an attempt at a shrug  'I wish I could help you, but he was just a man  Maybe about my age or a little older, clean-shaven, light-complected, dressed nice but not flashy, respectable-looking. I was hoping he'd put in a dollar, but he let on he didn't even notice me  Maybe he didn't. Judge not, that ye be not judged  Oh, and he was wearing dark glasses, those goggle kind like the hippies used to wear. Sort of unusual, I thought, a man like him on a day like this. It's not glary out or anything  Oh, thank you. Merry Christmas '

Max made sure the folded five-dollar bill cleared the chicken wire and came safely to rest on the coins he'd already thrown in  'You, too. Thanks for your help.'

His quarry was long gone by now, of course. Getting him tangled up with the lassie and her kettle had been an effective delaying tactic  But how in hell had the guy managed so neatly to give him the elbow at precisely the right moment? Max could have sworn he hadn't so much as glanced back to see that Max was after him.

He could have noticed Max before Max was aware of him, though  Cambridge Street rises in a fairly steep gradient from the river up to Cornhill. Max had used the elevated pedestrian walk to cross from the West End side to the Beacon Hill side before he'd started the climb  If the man had been looking back down while Max was descending the stairs, say, he could have spotted him easily enough. Max knew himself to be easily recognizable, though he'd never been able to figure out why.

It would have taken fairly good eyesight, but elderly people are apt to be farsighted, and the sunglasses might have helped, if they had prescription lenses in them. Perhaps the man's hearing was sharp, too, and he'd been listening for quick footsteps behind him. There'd been nothing wrong with his reflexes, either. That fast jab in the ribs was the sort of thing a man who could deliver a perfect karate chop in a moving train would be good at.

Max wondered. Had he actually been tracking a killer up Cambridge Street, in broad daylight and in full view of the Salvation Army?

## CHAPTER 15

Was it mere coincidence that the collision had occurred at the corner of Temple Street? Temple wasn't much of a thoroughfare, but it did lead up to the State House and thence, by a couple of short turns or a detour through the State House, to other parts of the Hill, to Beacon Street, or down to Charles Or, for that matter, to Joy Street.

Max had been on his way to Joy Street anyway He couldn't think where else to go at the moment. Furthermore, Joy Street was close to Tulip and the new apartment to which Sarah might by now have returned triumphant from her quest for the ultimate tea cosy. He turned up Temple.

That wasn't the least risky thing Max could have done. Like all the other streets on the Hill, Temple was barely wide enough for one lane of traffic and half-choked with parked cars. It was on the unfashionable side, too, where people weren't punctilious about taking in their trash cans. It also seemed to have a disproportionate number of unexpected alleys and dark cellars Max was glad Sarah had made him wear his muffler.

The muffler was a handsome one Aunt Emma had knitted

him for his birthday, of some featherweight but marvellously thick, bouncy yarn. It would make a useful cushion for his thorax if the man who was so good at commando tactics was around to try another whack. Max didn't want to be killed. He wanted to be around to see his mother's face when she unwrapped Sarah's Christmas present.

He kept to the middle of the street and walked fast, even for him. When he got safely to the top and around behind the State House, he took a deep breath When he pushed on to the intersection of Mount Vernon and Joy, he realized he needn't have worried. The man who'd knocked him into the kettle hadn't been lurking behind a trash can ready to pounce. He'd strolled on ahead and was just now entering a doorway a few houses down on Joy Street.

Pleasantly surprised to have done the right thing more or less by accident, Max took careful note of which house it was, then ducked back around the corner Once the man was inside, he sauntered along to the house and up the stairs to the front door. His first impulse was to look for Ashbroom's name on one of the doorbells. It wasn't there, so he pushed a bell at random, hoping whoever heard the ring would be foolhardy enough to release the buzzer.

The person who belonged to the bell was either smart or absent, so he tried the first floor. This time he got no mere buzz but a smashing redhead in tight green pants, high-heeled red sandals, and a voluminous but loosely knit green sweater with nothing under it except herself She was decked out to be somebody's Christmas present, he realized She must have thought it was the intended recipient who'd rung her bell or she wouldn't have been so quick to answer in person.

Max expected to be given either the bum's rush or a price list, but the redhead surprised him again.

'Hello. Eddie sent you, didn't he? Come in, quick, and tell me what's happening. All I can get out of that damned hospital is a recording that keeps saying no visitors except next of kin and the switchboard is not equipped to handle personal inquiries '

'I don't suppose it is,' said Max, following her into the apartment before she had a chance to change her mind 'It's just as well you couldn't get through. Ed Ashbroom's in a sticky position just now, as you must have heard '

'It was on the news about his wife being dead, if that's what you mean. Couldn't have happened to a nicer person If you're a cop or a reporter, I didn't say that And before I say anything else, may I ask with whom I'm having the pleasure?'

'Jeremy Kelling's nephew Max.' That had worked well enough last night It seemed to be working now. 'You know Jem, don't you?'

'We haven't met, but Eddie's told me a lot about him He sounds like a real blast '

'Jem's that and then some And you're Miss Moriston, of course ' At least that was the name on her bell. 'I'm just back from visiting Jem at the hospital,' he added when she didn't say she was not Miss Moriston.

'Did you see Eddie, too? How's he doing?'

Max should perhaps have corrected Miss Moriston's natural misapprehension as to which hospital he'd been visiting, but he didn't 'As well as can be expected,' sounded like a safely ambiguous reply

'Has anybody else been to see him?' she asked sharply.

The police, no doubt. Max dodged that one, too. 'They really are being very strict about visitors.'

'What for? Nobody's really buying that garbage about Russian terrorists, are they?'

'Aren't you?'

'You've got to be kidding,' she snorted, then looked as if she wished she hadn't. 'I don't know. Should I?'

He shrugged. 'I'm keeping an open mind. You know Ed Ashbroom a lot better than I do. Or so I've been given to understand.'

'I'll bet you have.'

Miss Moriston cast a long, thoughtful glance from Max's well-grouped features to the hand-tailored suit that showed beneath the no less handsome tweed overcoat he was unbuttoning. Then she rearranged her see-through sweater for greater ease of viewing and sauntered over to a bar some evil-minded interior decorator had caused to be made from what must once have been a perfectly respectable rosewood melodeon. Max wondered if it was the high-heeled sandals or whether she always walked like that.

'Care to join me in a spot of Christmas cheer?' she purred in a voice that matched her sweater.

'I don't want to dampen your holiday spirit,' Max replied, 'but it might be a little early to start celebrating '

'What do you mean? Hey, Eddie's not going to die, is he? He can't! Not now  He hasn't even signed the—what am I talking about? Don't pay any attention to me. I'm all upset.'

Miss Moriston poured herself a cocktail glass of gin, added a careful two drops of vermouth, said perfunctorily, 'You're not going to join me?' and drank about half the glassful.

After a while, she got her breath back. 'I'm crazy about Eddie  This has been a terrible experience for me  Be sure and tell him that when you see him again, won't you? Tell him I'm all to pieces  When are you going back to the hospital?'

'That depends on a number of things,' Max told her 'Maybe I'll have a small Scotch. No, you sit down and pull yourself together  I'll fix it myself. Where's the ice? Through here?'

'No!'

Before Max could open the door that might or might not lead to a kitchen, she was in front of him, blocking the way with her sweater heaving

'Don't go in there  It's a mess. I've been too upset to bother about cleaning the place up. Look, I don't want to seem inhospitable, but maybe you'd better take a rain check, huh?

I feel terribly faint all of a sudden. I've got to lie down for a while. It's the shock You understand, don't you?'

'Sure, I understand.'

Max could have sworn he understood perfectly, but then he heard the front door slam and saw Miss Moriston snap to attention.

'Was that somebody going out? I thought—oh '

Her bay window looked out on the street. Max could see the front steps and a man going down them. His face was turned away, but part of a wraparound sunglass lens was visible between the pulled-down brim of his dark felt hat and the turned-up collar of his dark wool overcoat. Max recognized the overcoat It was the one he'd chased all the way from Cambridge Street Now he didn't understand at all, so he bade Miss Moriston a fast goodbye and left.

His man went back up Joy to Mount Vernon, on to Walnut, then down again on Chestnut. If he knew he was being followed, he made no sign He did put on a burst of speed going down Chestnut, but the steep grade makes it hard not to, so Max didn't know whether to count that or not In any event, the man kept going at a brisk but not hurried pace across Charles and on towards the river, until he reached a house Max recognized This was where he'd collected Marcia Whet, her bustle, her boa, and her stuffed pheasant the night before.

Could the man be Gerry Whet, back from Nairobi? If so, what had Mr Whet been up to, sneaking out of Miss Moriston's door? This was turning out to be quite an interesting promenade

There were elegant homes on this part of the Hill, and Whet's was by no means the least of these. He, or whoever it was, eschewed the impressive front entrance and walked around under a portico, out of sight For want of a better idea, Max went to the front and rang the bell The same elderly maid who'd held Marcia's cape the night before answered his ring.

'I'd like to see Mr Whet,' he told her.

'Oh ' The maid devoted a fair space of time to examining Max up and down through the various levels of her trifocals, then conceded him a grim nod. 'You're Mr—er—the gentleman who took Mrs Whet to the party.'

'That's right Jem Kelling's nephew Max.'

The man of a thousand in-laws. Again he'd said the magic words. The maid actually smiled.

'Oh, Mr Jem. He's a great friend of the family. How's his hip?'

'Sore I just came from seeing him at the hospital You can imagine what he's doing to the morale over there.'

'Keeps those nurses hopping, I'll bet. Come in, Mr Max Here, let me take your coat I'll go see if Mr Whet's up yet How did you know he was home? I didn't, myself, till I went to draw the blinds this morning and found him asleep in his own bed I didn't have the heart to wake him Isn't it awful about Mrs Whet? I'm glad it's you and not me that's got to tell him.'

'Tell him what?' Max felt something like panic rising 'I mean, what was your latest report from the hospital?'

'Just that she's still on the critical list and they're doing the best they can. I was hoping you'd heard something more encouraging '

'I wish I had How long ago was it that you looked in on Mr Whet?'

'About half past nine, if you want the truth. I was awfully late getting around to my chores this morning I'd stayed up late to see if they'd broadcast anything more about Mrs Whet and the rest of them on the news. Then I couldn't get to sleep for thinking about it. They're great friends, you know, my folks and the Tolbathys We have them here a lot And Mr Jem, too, as I guess I don't have to tell you He's a great one to liven up a dinner party. Him and his stories! Mr Whet says Mr Jem's the only man he'll trust Mrs Whet with while he's away because Mr Jem could never stick with one woman long enough to be dangerous. Though I s'pose I shouldn't have said that in front of you.'

'Why not? I've said worse to his face Jem's more talk than action anyway, if you want my personal opinion '

Max glanced at his watch. Getting on for one o'clock There'd been plenty of time for Whet to have dressed and slipped out of the house, done whatever the hell he was up to, come back just now, and slipped back into bed again.

The maid must have thought Max was giving her a hint 'Well, I'd better go see if he's stirring yet. It's high time, anyway He'll be cross with me for not getting him up sooner, with Mrs Whet so sick and him not even knowing. You don't mind, do you, Mr Max?'

Inferring that she meant his being manoeuvred into breaking the news about Mrs Whet, which in fact gave him a decent excuse to be there, Max said no, he didn't mind. She went off more amiably than she'd come, leaving him in sole possession of what must be the Whets' customary sitting-room Through an open door, he could see a formal living-room done up in pale yellows and looking chilly on this raw, overcast December day. The white poinsettias lined up on a white marble mantelpiece did nothing to cosy up the effect

In here, though, the slipcovers were bright, the poinsettias red, the mantel trimmed with golden balls and red velvet ribbons Lots of photographs stood around in silver frames: of Marcia young and ethereal behind a cloud of wedding tulle; of Marcia holding a baby with two toddlers leaning against her knees; of Marcia in a long dress and corsage beside a daughter wearing what was no doubt the same wedding veil, another daughter in a bridesmaid's gown and floppy hat, the Gerry Whet of Jem's picture in morning clothes; his son beside him, another Comrade in the making and the image of his father; and another young man looking correct, happy, terrified, and obviously the new son-in-law

There were later photographs of Marcia Whet as Max had

met her, matronly now but still charming, surrounded by an ever-growing brood of young adults, children, and yet more babies. Gerry Whet was with her in many of the pictures A family man, one would have said, well pleased with himself, his wife, his children, his grandchildren, his lot in life. And with reason, one would have thought, looking at these happy captured memories in this agreeable room of this handsome house at this eminently acceptable address No money worries here, one would deduce, knowing roughly what it must cost to maintain an establishment of this size in Boston nowadays

Establishment That made Max think Where was the greenhouse? He was wondering about Whet and his wolf-bane when the maid came back with a decanter of sherry and a plate of biscuits on a silver tray

'Mr Whet says he'll be with you in a few minutes, if you'd care to wait He's getting up now I'll have coffee ready in a few minutes, if you'd prefer that to sherry.'

'Sherry will be fine, thank you '

This appeared to be Offer-Bittersohn-a-Drink Day He might as well take this one before the maid changed her mind as Ashbroom's Miss Moriston had done The decanter, he noticed, was Waterford. Sarah had Waterford decanters, too She'd used them at the boarding-house to distract her lodgers' minds from the cheapness of the sherry. That wasn't the case here Like everything else of the Whets', the sherry was quietly expensive and in excellent taste

He was tired. He hadn't realized how tired, until now. The superb wine, the serene room, the comfortable chair, the noise of the traffic on Storrow Drive that penetrated this well-insulated fastness only as a far-off, steady roaring like the waves on the beach back at Ireson's Landing; all these were well on their way towards lulling him to sleep when Gerald Whet appeared, freshly shaven and moderately rested, very much the master of the house in a brocaded robe over an open-necked shirt and dark trousers.

'So you're Jem Kelling's nephew?' he remarked as they shook hands 'Max, eh? I've been trying to place you.'

'Husband of Sarah who's the only begat of the late Walter,' Max told him. He was damned if he'd call her 'relict of the late Alexander' 'My name's Bittersohn, actually. I filled in for Jem last night as your wife's escort to the Tolbathy's party, because Jem had a fall and broke his hip in case you haven't heard. Your wife started introducing me around as Jem's nephew and that made it easy for people to fit me in, so we just kept doing it They all knew Jem, of course.'

'I should think so! Good Lord, how did they manage to hold the party without him? What happened, Max? Did he slip on the ice?'

'No, he fell downstairs rushing out to buy himself a false beard for the party '

Gerald Whet laughed. 'That sounds like Jem Where is the old coot? Phillips House, I suppose The Comrades will have to send him an appropriate get-well message You wouldn't happen to know where we might find a stuffed octopus, for instance? A really big one? Jem's not in too much pain, I hope?'

'He claims he is I've just been to see him.'

'And he sent you here with a message for Marcia to rush over and sponge his fevered brow with a pitcherful of martinis, no doubt. I'm afraid I can't tell you where she is at the moment Haven't seen her myself, as a matter of fact She may have gone out on some errand or other, thinking I'd want to sleep off my jet lag I only got back from Nairobi about three o'clock this morning. I was rather surprised not to meet her getting back from the party. What time did you drop her off? Or did she spent the night with Hester Tolbathy?'

'She and Hester both spent the night at Bexhill Hospital, I'm afraid,' Max told him.

'What do you mean? Was there an accident to the train? Marcia isn't badly hurt?'

'There was a contrived accident, but that's not the real

problem. Your wife, like almost everyone else on the train, got sick to her stomach from eating contaminated caviar They were all hauled off in ambulances.'

'Caviar?' Whet shook his head. 'I can't believe it How bad is she?'

'It's a bad situation altogether ' Max wasn't liking this 'Edith Ashbroom is dead. So is John Wripp, though he seems to have died mostly from shock and injuries he got in a bad fall when the train stopped short Wouter Tolbathy is also dead '

'Wouter? But he hates caviar '

'That so? Nobody mentioned it before However, Wouter didn't die from the caviar He died from a smashed windpipe '

'My God,' gasped Whet 'You don't mean that commando trick Obed Ogham—no, that's impossible '

'The police are calling Wouter's death an accident. They haven't yet come up with a plausible explanation of how such an accident could have occurred, as far as I know I expect they'll think of something if they get leaned on hard enough by the district attorney '

Whet shook his head and murmured 'My God' again 'But you still haven't told me how Marcia is '

'Your maid tells me the hospital called early this morning to say she'd been put on the critical list, along with several others Apparently there's been no significant change since then, or the hospital would have let you know '

'What's the number out there? Do you have it?'

'No, and it wouldn't do you any good. The switchboard isn't accepting any calls. They are, however, letting immediate family members visit the patients, so I suggest you go out there in person. Have your maid fix you a quick bite, why don't you, and throw on some clothes. I'll get my car and pick you up in fifteen minutes.'

'Can you make it sooner? How could I eat with Marcia— oh, my God, what am I going to tell the children?'

'You'd better get the facts before you try to tell them anything, hadn't you? They must have heard the story on the news already '

'They can't have, or they'd have been trying to reach me already. The whole crew are up at our mountain lodge this weekend, skiing. We have no radio or television up there.'

'No newspapers either?' Not having the daily paper delivered was to Max the ultimate deprivation He could never figure out why people who could afford every luxury were willing to forgo such a basic necessity of life.

But Whet shook his head again 'Oh, no, they wouldn't bother Max, if you mean it about driving me out to Bexhill, I'd be eternally grateful. I don't keep a car in the city myself, and it's a hell of a distance by cab.'

They couldn't help it, Max had decided some time ago It must come from eating all those fishcakes and baked beans. 'I'll be back as fast as I can,' he assured Whet 'My car's just over on Charles Street '

Max didn't wait for the maid to let him out. She must be busy in the kitchen; he could smell coffee brewing He hoped she'd manage to get a cup into her employer before Whet left the house. This wasn't going to be any pleasure trip

## CHAPTER 16

Gerald Whet showed no sign of wanting to talk on the way out to Bexhill. His silence could have been due to depression or exhaustion, or to avoid the strain of having to keep up an act. Max was still keeping an open mind

Whet had on a badly wrinkled and rather dirty Burberry, with a shapeless Irish tweed hat on his head. No doubt these were what he'd travelled in. They made him look exactly like a worn-out passenger who's just come off a long plane ride,

and Max would have liked to know whether Whet had had
that thought in mind when he put them on again.

It could simply have been that the garments were ready to
hand when he was rushing to get dressed, or that he'd got so
used to wearing them on his prowls through the pyrethrum
fields during the past few weeks that he'd donned them
automatically. In time of stress some familiar garment can
serve as a kind of security blanket. If Whet was really just off
the plane from Nairobi, if he really loved his wife all that
much, if he was really as worried and scared as he appeared
to be, then maybe he'd needed to grab at any scrap of comfort
he could find

On the other hand, Whet could have worn the Burberry to
keep Max Bittersohn from seeing him in a felt hat and city
overcoat; because he knew perfectly well Max Bittersohn
had been playing games all over Beacon Hill with a man
dressed in that same conventional garb, and that Max had
been led to Whet's house by that same man

Maybe the man had been Whet himself. Maybe it had
been Edward Ashbroom  Maybe it had been Miss Moriston's kid brother dressed in Ashbroom's clothes. Who the
hell knew? Maybe Max had been decoyed to Whet's house
simply because it was a handy place to lure somebody
Maybe Ashbroom had assumed Whet was still in Nairobi
and therefore he wouldn't be getting a Comrade into trouble
if he used the place to shake Bittersohn. Or maybe Ashbroom
had known Whet was there, and was deliberately trying to
make trouble for him.

Maybe the guy in the overcoat had been reading Miss
Moriston's gas meter and galloped off to Whet's next because he figured he'd cadge lunch off the maid. Bah, humbug  Max glanced over at Whet, who had his chin buried in
the collar of the Burberry and his eyes fixed on the road.

'How was your flight from Nairobi?'

'Long, boring, uncomfortable.' Whet spoke without taking his eyes from the road. 'As one would expect '

'You travelled first class, I suppose.'

'What for? Both ends of the plane go to the same place '

It was an argument Max himself would have used He found himself liking Whet, though it wasn't the professional thing to do. 'What route did you take?'

'Cairo to London We were late getting out of Heathrow, naturally. Then there was some kind of flap on going through customs and I had to kick around there for an extra hour or so '

'Oh I wondered how you managed to arrive at such an ungodly hour '

'One can generally count on getting fouled up somewhere along the line And what a homecoming! Wouter dead, Marcia poisoned on Hester's caviar at Hester's party Max, I simply can't believe this Damn it, Tom Tolbathy practically goes over and catches those sturgeon himself It's just not possible Hester served bad caviar.'

'The official position at the moment is that the caviar was deliberately laced at the cannery with colchicine '

'Colchicine?'

'It's used to treat gout.'

Max repeated what Jem's nurse had told him. Gerald Whet looked more interested than dismayed.

'Colchicine used to treat gout That's something I hadn't known '

'I suppose it's a little out of your line '

'Quite Tomato worms don't get gout Nice if they did, I suppose.'

'Do you know of any plant poisons that would produce those same symptoms?'

'Plant poisons?' Now the alarm had been sounded Whet was alert, and wary 'Why yes Now that you mention it, I can think of several Pyrethrum, for instance, though I should think one would have to take an enormous amount of it to do any real damage There have been poisonings from insecticides containing pyrethrum, but those are generally caused not by the pyrethrum itself but the petroleum distillates used in the base I suppose I should be thankful I was bucketing around on that damned plane instead of being at the party. At least I have an alibi, for what that's worth Though if Marcia—God, what a thing to come home to at Christmas!'

He fell silent again and didn't rouse himself until Max had stopped the car in the hospital parking lot Then he stirred, as though he might have been asleep.

'Are we there? You don't know Marcia's room number, I don't suppose?'

'They'll tell us at the desk If we can get in,' Max added, looking at the guards around the various entrances.

Whet set his jaw. 'We'll get in.'

For such a bland-looking man, Whet could be remarkably forceful, Max found. He overpowered two guards with a few softly spoken words. The receptionist didn't even ask for identification before she gave him Mrs Whet's room number.

'E-2, down this corridor and turn to the left. We've had to squeeze in the emergency patients wherever we could, but we're monitoring them very carefully '

'I should damn well hope so,' Whet answered, but he was already well on his way when he said it. Max tagged at his heels trying to look like an anxious son-in-law. In fact, he did feel genuine concern for the woman who'd been so jolly a companion, and he was surprisingly relieved when the floor nurse on E had somewhat reassuring news.

'Mrs Whet's showing a little improvement. We've taken her off the critical list and she's able to take liquids by mouth '

'What liquids?' Whet asked sharply.

'Just a little weak tea so far, but we're going to try her on orange juice later. Mrs Whet's being a very cooperative patient. Right in here.'

A pathetic caricature of the buxom charmer Max had squired to the Tolbathys' lay on the high bed with an intravenous tube in her arm. When Max caught the look on Gerald Whet's face as he bent over his wife, he decided maybe he ought to go over and talk to the nurse for a while.

'Are you Mrs Whet's son?' the nurse asked him

'No, I'm the guy who took her to the party.'

'You were on that train? Boy, are you the lucky one That caviar must have been loaded. It's a wonder everybody didn't die. How come you aren't sick?'

'I didn't eat any caviar. Was it really that bad?'

'The lab reports were horrendous.'

'But why colchicine? That's not a common poison, surely? I'd never heard of it before '

'Neither had I, if you want the truth I mean, not as a poison Of course many drugs are dangerous if you exceed the prescribed dosage. And colchicine has an unusually narrow margin of safety, which is something else I hadn't realized until the pharmacist put out the word. I suppose it was a case of using what was available, but don't you think gout medicine was a funny thing to be kicking around a caviar cannery? Though I suppose they get rheumatism from the cold and damp. At least I should think it would be cold and damp. My aunt's a sardine packer up in Maine, and she wears heavy socks and rubber boots to work all the time. She says it's kind of fun when you get used to it '

'Wearing rubber boots and heavy socks?'

'No, packing sardines I guess there's quite an art to it, like doing jigsaw puzzles How the heck did I get off on sardines? Punchy, I guess I went off duty yesterday at six o'clock. They called me back about ten last night when the ambulances began rolling in crammed to the tailgates, and I haven't sat down since except for a cup of coffee now and then to keep me awake This hospital's not equipped to handle large-scale emergencies, but what could we do? You can't dillydally around shipping poison cases off to other hospitals. They could be dead by the time they got there '

'Couldn't you have got some nurses in from another facility?'

'Where, for instance? They're all understaffed, same as us '

'You must be dead on your feet by now,' Max sympathized

'If I could find an empty bed, you'd better believe I'd crawl into it,' the nurse replied 'Oh well, I expect they'll be letting some of us go home pretty soon. We do have some Red Cross emergency personnel coming in to take up the slack, and things are beginning to quiet down They've even released some of the patients.'

'Who, for instance?'

'Let's see. A list just came around ' She fished through the papers on the desk and found it 'Thomas Tolbathy He's the man who gave the party, right?'

'That's right. Tolbathy wasn't very sick, was he? He told me back at the train that he'd only tasted the caviar '

'I think it was mostly shock and nervous upset in his case No wonder, poor guy. I'd hate to be in his shoes right now.'

'How's his wife?'

'Still guarded And the brother was DOA, of course, I expect you know about that.'

'I ought to. I was one of the guys who found him.'

Max decided he'd better toss the nurse a nugget or two of gossip himself, if he wanted to keep her talking She wouldn't be so chatty about her patients, no doubt, if she weren't so exhausted herself. Perhaps she felt that his having been at the party gave him some kind of special status He pushed his luck

'What about the official cause of Wouter Tolbathy's death? Has it been anounced yet?'

'Fractured trachea. Really freaky.' The nurse rubbed the back of her left hand across her eyes. 'I think I need another cup of coffee. Care to join me?'

'Sure, if it's not against the rules.'

'It's okay if I say so. I'm floor nurse, I think. We're all so beat by now we don't know who's what.'

She led him into a small kitchen where a glass coffee maker was keeping hot on an electric plate, poured out two mugfuls, helped herself to milk and a great deal of sugar. 'How do you want yours?'

'Black for me, please.'

Max took his mug and sat down beside her on one of the stools pulled up to a plastic laminated counter The coffee tasted better than he'd thought it would, or perhaps he'd needed it more than he'd realized. He let the nurse get a few sips into her before he asked another question

'Who else has been released?'

'Ellen Oliphant, Jessica Puffer.' Names that meant nothing to Max 'Quent Durward We read a book about him at school. Different one, I suppose Donald Dork What a name! Here's another, Nehemiah Billingsgate, Abigail Billingsgate His wife, I imagine Edward Ashbroom Obed Ogham '

'Ogham? When did they let him go?'

'Early this morning About half past eight, I think None too soon, in my opinion Oops, are you a friend of his?'

'Is anybody?'

The nurse laughed and choked on her coffee 'Not around here,' she managed to say after Max had kindly slapped her on the back 'I can't remember when we've had a worse pest on the floor When they brought him up, he was moaning and carrying on as if he was ready for the last rites Half an hour later, he acted like one of those jerky get-well cards where the patient's ripping the pants off every nurse who comes within grabbing reach. Would you believe he even tried to put the moves on me?'

She must have been at least fifty and no doubt somebody's mother. 'I told him to keep his hands to himself or I'd bop him with a full urinal.'

'Too bad you didn't,' said Max 'Was Ogham really

poisoned? I saw him being sick back at the train, but I thought it might have been from the liquor He'd had an awful lot to drink. Do you know whether each patient's stomach contents were analysed separately after they'd been pumped out?'

'I couldn't say for sure, but I'm inclined to think not. We were really swamped, as I said Anyway, once the diagnosis had been made there was nothing we could do but treat them symptomatically regardless of how much or how little poison they'd swallowed. There wouldn't have been much point in doing a separate quantitative analysis on each patient I mean, they're either going to get better or—'

'Sure, I understand,' Max said quickly 'I just wondered Did you take care of Ashbroom?'

'No, he wasn't on my floor We had Mr Durward, though He was a character We couldn't make him out One time you'd go into his room and he'd be nice as pie The next time, he'd act as if he didn't know you were there '

'He probably didn't My wife's uncle claims he's legally blind and too vain to admit it Did Durward talk much about what happened? When he talked at all, I mean.'

'Oh yes. He asked about Mr Ogham and Mr Dork, I remember. He said they'd been talking together when the train crashed He wanted to know if they'd been killed in the wreck He wouldn't believe me when I tried to tell him there wasn't any wreck. But there wasn't, was there?'

'No, the train stopped suddenly and people got jolted around, that's all. Did Durward realize he'd been poisoned?'

'Not until we told him He thought it must have been escaping gas or something that made everybody sick '

'He did recall eating the caviar, though '

'Yes, and would you believe it, he was cross because he didn't get more. Apparently he and these friends of his had been off in a corner talking, and the waitress only passed the tray to them once. That must be why they were all able to leave this morning. But Mr Durward was quite miffed at having been stinted on the er derves. That's what a friend of mine calls them My husband says ordures. I told Mr Durward he ought to be glad he didn't eat more, because then he'd have got poisoned worse than he was already, but he only said, "*She* didn't know they were poisoned. That's no excuse for her to slight me " Can you beat that? Well, I'd better get back on the floor.'

She stuck her mug and Max's in a rack for the dishwasher and went out to the desk. Max decided he might as well leave If he tried prowling the corridors trying to interrogate patients, they'd only throw him out anyway

Through the open door of the room Marcia Whet was in, he could see her husband sitting in one of those wooden armchairs with bright plastic seats that are supposed to strike a cheery note in the sickroom He had the chair drawn up to the bed and was holding his wife's hand She appeared to be asleep. Max cleared his throat. Whet looked around, then he laid Marcia's hand tenderly back on the coverlet and came out into the corridor

'I suppose you'd like to get along, Max? Why don't you go ahead? I want to stay with Marcia.'

'How will you get back to Boston?'

Whet shrugged. 'One way or another, I suppose. I could beg a bed at the Tolbathys' if there's anybody around to ask. How's Tom, did you find out?'

'Doing fine, I gather. He's been released.'

'That's heartening news And Hester?'

'Her condition's still guarded, whatever that means.'

'Better than critical, surely.' Whet looked in at his wife, as if anxious to get back to her.

'Tell you what,' said Max, 'why don't I take a run over to the Tolbathys'? Tom will be glad to know you're back, and I can ask him about putting you up for the night.'

'Thank you, that's a kind thought Yes, I expect Tom might welcome some company later, with Hester still here and Wouter—God, I can't imagine one of those brothers without the other. Give him my best, won't you? Oh, and see if he could arrange transportation. I'm sure he's not up to driving himself.'

'Right. I'll either stop back or get a message to you.'

Max meant to say goodbye to his new friend the nurse, but she was rushing up the corridor with an IV bottle in her hand and a grim set to her mouth. This was no time for idle pleasantries. He went out and got into his car.

## CHAPTER 17

Max left the parking lot under the sombre stare of a state policeman who looked as if he'd missed his lunch and held Max Bittersohn personally responsible for keeping him from it. On the way in, he'd followed the H signs to the hospital Now, on the reasonable theory that this road must lead somewhere, Max turned left and kept going, until he reached an intersection To his relief, it looked familiar Yes, there sat and trim little catering shop. And there went Angie, putting a large carton into a station wagon with its tailgate down

Max hadn't intended to do more than honk and drive on, but Angie spotted him and waved so wildly that he slowed down and pulled into the drive

'How come you're hanging around the shop?' he asked her 'I thought you'd be off somewhere raking in the bucks.'

'Marge and Pam are doing a luncheon,' she explained. 'I'm trying to get ready for a big bash at the Masons' tonight Thank goodness nobody's cancelling, but they're all giving us strict orders not to serve any caviar. I understand it's already being recalled from the stores That's going to make poor Mr Tolbathy even sicker than he was last night, I'll bet. He's out of the hospital, did you know?'

'How did you find that out?'

'If you lived in Bexhill, you wouldn't have to ask. We get

all the news before it happens. Customers come in for rolls and stuff, and stop to pass the time of day You know how it is '

'I hadn't realized you sold food over the counter.'

'Oh, we have to. That's the only way we can meet our overhead when business slacks off in the catering department It's not always two affairs on the same day, you know. How's your wife?'

'Fine. How about selling me something to take home to her? Do you have time?'

'Sure I'm just trying to get some of tonight's stuff organized so it won't be a last-minute scramble. We do have a countergirl, but she's on her lunch break just now. Speaking of which, have you eaten?'

'Actually, no. I just came from driving Mrs Whet's husband out to the hospital You don't sell sandwiches and coffee, by any chance?'

'You could have quiche, or a Ploughman's lunch.'

'Ploughman's would be great '

Max went in and sat down at one of the little tables, rightly expecting to be served some excellent bread and cheese in the manner of a British pub, with perhaps some chutney and a ripe tomato on the side. He hadn't bargained for the tomato to be carved into the shape of a full-blown rose, but he supposed Angie couldn't help herself.

'Too bad I didn't know enough to pick up some beer,' he remarked, sniffing the crusty roll with due appreciation

Angie, who'd just brought another plateful to the table for herself, went back to the refrigerator and returned with a dark brown bottle

'We don't have a liquor licence, so this has to be on the house Merry Christmas '

'Shalom.'

They sipped their beer, then Max asked, 'Has there been anything on the grapevine about the husband of that woman who died?'

'Mr Ashbroom? Nothing special, as far as I know '

'Does he live around here?'

'Sure, right up the street. That great big yellow house on the hill, just down from the hospital. You must have come past it.'

'You mean the one with all the windows?'

'That's right. It's got a greenhouse built on. The Ashbrooms are really into gardening.'

'So my wife's uncle was telling me.'

Angie chewed on her bread and cheese for a moment, then said, 'Speaking of wives, I wonder when Mrs Ashbroom's funeral is going to be I hope they don't ask us to cater the back-to-the-house part. We're booked solid all week I hate doing funerals anyway '

'I should think the family would want to keep everything private, under the circumstances,' said Max.

'Unless it turns out to be a double feature,' Angie replied cynically 'Then maybe the heirs will feel like celebrating.'

'Who stands to inherit, do you know? Have the Ashbrooms any children?'

'She never had any. I couldn't say about him '

'That kind of guy, eh?'

'You couldn't prove it by me, but that's the scuttlebutt around town. Of course it may be just talk.'

Max didn't feel it was his place to resolve the speculation. Miss Moriston would take care of that angle, no doubt, provided Edward Ashbroom gave her a chance. He paid for his lunch, insisted on paying for Angie's, too, bought some buns and petits fours to take home to Sarah, and went on to the Tolbathys'.

Impeccably maintained as it was, the mansion looked somehow tacky in the daylight. The dingy effect must have been due to the trampled lawn and the bits of litter left by the many people who'd been milling around here last night. Even a thrown-away matchbook seemed like a deliberate insult. Max wished another snowstorm would come along and make it white again.

He didn't know whether or not he'd get an answer to his ring, but Mrs Rollo opened the door quite promptly.

'Good afternoon, sir. You're Mr Kelling's nephew, aren't you?'

'Yes,' he told her, since that was obviously his Open Sesame. 'Is Mr Tolbathy up to seeing me? I have messages for him from Jem and Mr Whet.'

'Mr Whet's back? He'll be glad to know that. Just a minute, I'll tell him you're here '

Mrs Rollo left Max in the reception hall and disappeared. He'd spied an Alfred Sisley landscape and was giving it a professional once-over when she came back.'

'He says for you to go right on up. Just turn left at the head of the stairs. You won't mind if I don't take you myself?'

'Not at all. You must be worn out from last night.'

Anyway, locating the master bedroom was no problem. It was the size of a bowling alley. Tom Tolbathy, in a high four-poster with an eight-foot canopy, looked pathetically insignificant. His face had no more colour than the old-fashioned white sheets with their heavy lace-trimmed edges, but he had strength enough to hold out a hand when Max went over to the bed.

'Hello, Max  Good of you to come '

'How are you feeling, Tom?'

'Not too bad. The doctor said I'd better take it easy for a while. What's this about Gerry Whet? How did he happen to get in touch with you? Did he call Jem from Nairobi?'

'No, he's home. Got in early this morning, he says  I've driven him out to the hospital and left him there. He sends his best and wonders if you could offer him a bed for tonight  He wants to stay near Marcia.'

'Of course  I'll be delighted to have him  I know exactly how Gerry feels. You didn't get any recent report on Hester, by chance?'

'According to the floor nurse, her condition's guarded but not critical They didn't sound too worried about her, if that's any consolation to you.'

'Right now, I'll snatch at anything How's Marcia? Did you see her?'

'Yes, and she's a little better They've taken her off the critical list and given her a cup of tea '

'Thank God for that! If Gerry'd come home and found her—he's pretty devastated as it is, I expect.'

'It was quite a jolt, certainly. He's as concerned for you as he is for his wife, I think He took it hard about your brother.'

'He would. Good old Gerry God, I still can't believe any of this. Now there's some nonsense being talked about some Russian's having poisoned the caviar They're howling about having to recall every blasted can we've sold '

'Will it affect you seriously if they do?'

'The firm, you mean? It could wipe us out, I suppose The caviar alone wouldn't matter so much, it's what would happen afterwards People are so leery about poison in food, you know Can't blame them of course And we're a small family concern. Never wanted to be anything more. Still don't. It wouldn't take much to send us to the wall. I can't seem to care about that now. But our great-grandfather started the business. I expect I wouldn't much like to be the one who finished it.'

'Assuming the business does keep going,' said Max, 'how will your brother's death affect its day-to-day operation? If that's not an improper question.'

'Oh, it's not improper.' Tolbathy put a puzzled stress on the last word, as if he wondered why Max hadn't said 'irrelevant' instead.

'Wouter will be missed, of course. My brother was—oh, everyone's favourite uncle. Nobody ever cared what he did, we simply enjoyed having him around. As far as our actual operations are concerned, I don't suppose his absence will matter a whit  Neither would mine, if it comes to that  My sons would just step in and carry on. They do most of the work as it is, these days '

'Your sons weren't at the party last night.'

'No, they've gone skiing with the younger Whets. This was strictly for Hester's and my old crowd. The family were all together for a big celebration at Thanksgiving, you know, and we were planning another at Christmas  Wouter was always the life and soul—' Tom couldn't get any farther.

'I'm sorry I never got to know Wouter,' said Max

'You'd have liked him.' Tom blew his nose. 'Everybody did.'

'You're sure of that?'

'What? Oh, I see  Max, you do realize the police are calling Wouter's death an accident?'

'Yes, and I expect you yourself realize they're doing it for the same reason they're calling your poisoned caviar a Russian plot  They figure it's what you want  Is it?'

'God, what a question '

Tolbathy sighed and didn't say any more for a while. Then he shook his head, slowly, as if it hurt  'No, that's not what I want. One can't cover up wrongdoing. So we have to let them go ahead and find out which of my guests murdered Wouter and tried to poison the rest. That will salvage the firm, I expect, at God knows what cost in broken friendships and public humiliation.'

'If you did go along with a cover-up, there's always the chance you might not have many friends left to offend, after a while. Or any family to be humiliated  The kind of person who'd feed a deadly poison indiscriminately to a whole trainload of his alleged friends can't be overly concerned with the sanctity of human life. He's probably off someplace right now, buying himself a drink to celebrate and wondering what he should do for an encore.'

'All right, Max. I've said what you wanted me to say. Now what do you want me to do?'

'Make it plain to the police you don't want any favours but only the truth'

'They won't believe I mean it unless I can furnish some hard evidence They've already stuck their own necks out, don't forget.'

'I know. That's what I was building up to. We can't expect them to break their backs now looking for something they don't want to find, so what we have to do is hand them something they can't turn down We might start with the colchicine. Know anybody other than Wouter who takes gout medicine? Do you know where he got his? Do you know a pharmacist who could tell us where colchicine comes from? Damn, I ought to know that myself I worked in a drugstore when I was going to college. What I did mostly, though, was make banana splits.'

Tolbathy gave Max a wry hint of a smile 'If Wouter were here, he'd say the logical place to start would be with the banana splits.'

'And he'd have been right, like as not Would you happen to have a dictionary or an encyclopedia?'

'Certainly, in the library. Downstairs and to the right behind the staircase'

'Thanks.'

Max went on down He found the library: a handsome, high-ceilinged room with shell-carved arches over the tiers of bookshelves; antique globes sitting around on carved walnut stands and leather-topped tables; enormous folios laid open to show marvellous prints of locomotives from the era of the Old Ironsides and the Best Friend of Charleston; steel engravings of old railroad stations; maps of forgotten railways. It would have been a marvellous room to spend a day browsing in, but Max hadn't a day to spend on such a luxury. He spied a Webster's Unabridged on a wooden turntable and went directly to it.

'Colchicine: a poisonous alkaloid derived from the seeds and bulbs of the common colchicum. It is used in medicine and also to promote variations in plants, fruits, etc'

And there was a clean little line drawing of the colchicum itself. The name, it appeared, might have been derived from Colchis, the home of Medea, who, as the dictionary kindly reminded Max as if he hadn't already known, was a sorceress and poisoner of ancient legend. Colchicum, he learned, was also known as meadow saffron and looked like a crocus but bloomed in the fall instead of the springtime No doubt every damned plant breeder in Bexhill had a bucketful of colchicine powder and a meadowful of colchicum plants He slammed the book shut and went back upstairs.

'Do you know anybody around here who grows meadow saffron?' he asked Tom Tolbathy

'Meadow saffron? Is that what colchicine comes from?'

'That's what it says in the book. Apparently the plant's common enough.'

'I'm not much up on gardening, I'm afraid. Hester could tell you, or Dork. He knows all about—oh, God!'

'You and me both,' said Max.

There had been altogether too many gardeners on that train. The one he was wondering about right now was Gerald Whet. Why hadn't Tom's great pal shown any sign of recognition when Max had mentioned colchicine? It shouldn't take any high degree of brain power to link up colchicine with colchicum, not if your work involved you with poisonous plants.

Tom Tolbathy might be wondering about that, too He was sunk into his pillows, so pale that Max got scared.

'Shall I call the maid for you?' he asked.

'No, don't bother her I'm all right. It's my age, I suppose. Seventy-four last August. It's a long time to have lived. Too long, perhaps I've had it all my own way, up to now Nothing awful ever happened, except for the war and Cousin Bigelow getting killed. We were babies together, Wouter and Biggie and I. Now I'm all that's left.'

'You have your friends.'

'Yes, my luck's still holding there. Jem and Gerry and the rest of the Comrades  Biggie'd have been a Comrade, if he'd lived. Max, I can't handle this. Do whatever you think best. And help me to the bathroom before you go, if you'll be so kind.'

'Sure, glad to.'

Max got Tolbathy valeted and saw him safely back to bed.

'Sorry if I've worn you out.'

'Don't be,' said Tolbathy. 'You're doing the right thing Tell Gerry he's welcome to use the Volvo. I wouldn't trust Rollo to drive after dark. And for God's sake, make them keep Hester in the hospital till it's safe for her to come out. If I lost her, too—' Tolbathy couldn't finish.

## CHAPTER 18

'Hester's going to be fine,' said Max, hoping to God he was right, 'and so are you and so are your friends ' Those who weren't already dead, at any rate

'Look, I'm going to leave you to get some rest now, but before I go, I'd like to look around your brother's room. Since you say he had no enemies, we'll have to find some other reason for him to have been killed  Was he likely to have got involved with one of the Comrades, say, in what he thought was just a practical joke? According to Jem, you go in rather heavily for pulling gags on each other.'

'We do,' Tolbathy conceded, 'and I suppose he might Though Wouter wasn't exactly the—I'm not sure how to put this.'

Max tried to help him out. 'For instance, when I mentioned Jem's broken hip to your friend Whet this afternoon—this was before he knew anything about what happened on the train—Whet's first reaction was to get hold of a stuffed octopus and send it to Jem at the hospital. Would Wouter have been the man Whet would have asked to deliver the octopus, for instance?'

'Probably not,' Tom admitted 'Not that Wouter wouldn't have thought a stuffed octopus just the ticket, mind you. I'd go for it myself, if I were up to that sort of thing right now. The problem with Wouter, though, was that one could never be sure where anything he took a hand in might wind up. He'd get to thinking that if a stuffed octopus was good, a live octopus would be even better, and why not have it come into the room wearing pink ballet slippers and dancing the tango with itself? That proving not feasible, Wouter would build a hollow one six feet high with movable parts, get inside it, and prance into the room wiggling the legs and flashing the eyeballs, and scare poor Jem into thinking the DT's had finally caught up with him '

Tolbathy actually managed to smile 'I must say the idea is not without a certain mad charm Wouter's projects seldom were.'

'Could your brother in fact have built a mechanical octopus?'

'Oh yes, easily Wouter had an incredible knack for that sort of thing. One of our grandsons is caught up in this Dungeons and Dragons craze just now, so Wouter built him a dragon as his Christmas present It breathes real fire '

'My God!'

'It's only sparks from some kind of ratchet thing and a red light in the throat that runs on batteries, but the effect is quite amazing. And it does the smoke and fume thing, of course. Wouter managed that with sulphur '

'How big is this dragon?'

'Five feet long or so. Wouter wanted to make it really dragon-sized, but Hester managed somehow to curb his enthusiasm. Woottie's room at school's only about ten feet square and already crammed to the ceiling with heaven knows what. You'll see the dragon in Wouter's workroom.

He lives—lived—in the suite over the kitchen wing. Go straight down the hall past the staircase, turn right at the arch, then straight through the door at the end. It won't be locked. We've never locked ourselves away from one another.'

Tom Tolbathy wasn't looking at Max, or at anything in particular. His eyes were bleak, fixed on a future without a brother who could build fire-breathing dragons. Max left him with his grief and went to find Wouter's rooms As he opened the connecting door that had never been kept locked, something growled.

It turned out to be Rollo

'Don't worry,' Max told him in the same tone he'd have used to conciliate a hostile dog. 'It's okay. Mr Tolbathy told me to come and have a look around '

Rollo didn't say anything, only jerked his head Max took that for an invitation and went in.

This must have been Wouter's sitting-room Hester, or somebody, had clearly devoted thought and care to decorating it comfortably in the discreet browns and rough-textured fabrics men are deemed to prefer. Wouter had added a few homey touches of his own

An articulated skeleton was stretched out on the sofa, modestly clad in a red flannel nightshirt with a monogram on the bosom, its skull cosily propped on a ruffled pink satin pillow. An avocado plant some seven feet high had its pot mounted on roller skates and its branches festooned with strings of gilded peanuts. These could have been intended as holiday decorations, but now that he'd had a glimpse of Wouter's modus operandi, Max thought they were more likely snacks for visiting squirrels with expensive tastes

The next room had been designed as a bedroom. Here again, the decorator had wrought in vain. Bed and dresser had been shoved aside to make room for a workbench, a power saw, a lathe, and a vast number of tools. There among the drills and hammers stood a handsome green dragon with a bright yellow belly and tasteful orange necktie, its upper scales subtly shaded from turquoise to chartreuse

Rollo, it was clear, took an avuncular interest in the dragon. He cranked it up and gave Max a demonstration. Sure enough, noxious fumes spewed forth from the nostrils, smoke curled around its head, an illuminated tongue darted flamelike from its scarlet-lined mouth, sparks flew as the ratchet created a wonderful rattling roar

The dragon was mounted on red wooden wheels and had, as one might have expected, a string to pull it by Rollo trundled it around the room, proud as a two-year-old with a new Christmas toy, while the dragon snorted and fumed and sparked in a manner that could not fail to delight the young sophisticates at Wootie's boarding school

'Ain't that somethin'?' Rollo demanded

Max said it sure was, and Rollo's heart was won. 'Want to see the trains?'

'Wouldn't miss 'em for anything. Where are they?'

'Through here '

Tom had certainly done his brother proud in the matter of space There was yet another room beyond the dragon's lair This was by far the largest, and it was wholly given over to a vast, complex electric train setup

Wouter hadn't missed a trick He'd created mountains with tunnels under them, rivers with trestles over them, quaintly picturesque country villages, big cities surrounded by realistically depressing urban sprawl There was a skyscraper with a window washer dangling against its mirrored side, capable of being raised and lowered from floor to floor on his tiny scaffolding. There was a fast-food restaurant with miniature chickens going in empty-winged at one door and coming out the other carrying little paper takeout bags. Max wondered a bit uncomfortably what Wouter had imagined might be inside the bags.

There were depots, roundhouses, shuntlines, switches galore. Rollo started flipping levers at a tremendous console.

Lights blinked, whistles blew, passenger and freight trains rushed over the trestles and through the tunnels, up the mountains and down the valleys Cars got coupled and uncoupled, shunted off, picked up by other trains, hustled away again around and around the tracks

Everything moved, it seemed The chickens marched in and out of the restaurant, the junk of the dumps got picked up and swung around by cranes, a steam shovel at a building site snapped at piles of sand, then dumped its gritty mouthfuls on other piles. This must be great fun for people who liked to pull switches and watch so much energy being expended to so little effect

Max could imagine Wouter standing there fiddling with the controls, admiring those insane chickens pecking their way in and out of the shop He'd have been wearing those engineering clothes, no doubt, that he'd had on when Max and Tom found him lying dead in the engine cab A duplicate suit was hanging on the back of the door Maybe Wouter had owned separate sets for big and little trains Or maybe this one was for visitors

'Did many of the Tolbathys' friends come to play trains with Wouter?' he asked Rollo.

'You betcha. They'd be lined up around the tracks sometimes three deep, singin' "Casey Jones" an' "The Runaway Train," greasin' up their tonsils with a jug o' martinis an' sendin' me downstairs for another one. Cripes, we had some great ol' times up here '

Pensively, Rollo dropped off a refrigerator car alleged to belong to the C&O Line and had it picked up by a passing Bangor & Aroostook freight, all from his control panel on the far side of the room.

'How do you do that?' Max asked him.

'Like this,' Rollo began his switching routine again.

'I mean, how do the cars get hitched and unhitched? My cousin had an electric train when we were kids, but he had to hook the cars on and off by hand.'

Rollo gave Max a haughtly glance 'Baby stuff All right for you kids, maybe These here's an old set. They used to be hand-couplin', but Wouter put electromagnetic solanoids in 'em. Wait a second.'

He flipped a master switch The trains, the cranes, even the marching chickens came to an abrupt halt Then he left the room Through the open doors, Max watched Rollo pick his way around the dragon and go to stand in the farthest doorway with his hands in his pockets, making a great show of doing nothing whatever. All at once, the trains started up again

'Wouter used to do that,' he chortled 'Never showed nobody the trick, neither.'

He probably wouldn't have had to Max had already guessed it: simply a hand-held remote control switch such as any number of people use nowadays to open their garage doors or turn on their television sets

'Wouter rigged it all,' Rollo boasted 'These here is mostly trains that belonged to their father, some of 'em, or to Tom an' Wouter when they was kids. Wouter put in all the switches hisself. Put 'em in the cranes an' such, too Even put 'em in the chickens so's they can pick up them little bitty bags an' put 'em down again '

'Good God! Wouter must have been a wizard '

'Yup. Wasn't much Mr Wouter couldn't do, once he put his mind to it Wasn't much he wouldn't put his mind to, neither '

'I can well believe that,' said Max with his eyes on the chickens. He'd just put his mind to something, also.

'Tell me, Rollo, did Wouter ever do odd jobs for his friends? Repairing their trains, anything like that?'

Rollo made a fair attempt at not understanding what Max was getting at. 'What would he want to take in odd jobs for? Mr Wouter had enough on 'is hands right here, didn't he?'

'But didn't they ever ask him? Look, let me put it this way. If you owned a train setup like this, say, and you wanted a

crane rigged up so it would dump sand like his, would you
have asked Wouter Tolbathy to wire it up for you?'

'H'nh.' Rollo made a choking noise that could have been
a laugh going down the wrong way. 'Not so's you'd notice
it.'

'But why not? You said yourself he could do anything '

'That's why I wouldn't ask 'im. See, Mr Wouter was awful
inventive. What I'm gettin' at is, he'd be glad to do you a
favour, but by the time he got through doin' it, you wouldn't
know if your crane was goin' to pick up dirt or play "The
Wreck o' the Old Ninety-Seven" or fry you a mess o'
fresh-caught trout '

'I get you '

Then it would appear to be unanimous  Nobody would
ever have trusted Wouter Tolbathy as far as they could have
thrown him, not because he was disobliging or lacking in
skill, but because he could never have resisted the urge to
make the job more interesting.

On the other hand, his great-nephew Woottie was fixated
on dragons, and for his namesake, Wouter had produced not
a gryphon or a wyvern or a camelopard but a perfectly
ordinary run-of-the-mill dragon. All one would have had to
do would have been to give him an assignment that was
totally mad to begin with, and he'd have been quite amen-
able to carry it out as requested  And, Max suspected,
Wouter had done exactly that  But for whom?

## CHAPTER 19

Jem had told Max that Dork, the man with the hangnail, was
a close neighbour of Tolbathy—close in Bexhill terms, anyway. Since Dork had been released at the same time as Tom,
the odds were he'd be at home in bed, too. Max decided not
to risk phoning to find out whether Dork was in a mood for

visitors. It would be harder to keep out a visitor who was already on the doorstep. He got directions from Mrs Rollo and went.

Dork's house presented an interesting contrast to the Tolbathy's dignified, somewhat austere Federal mansion This place must have been planned by a designer of cuckoo clocks back when the Victorians were in full cry after the gothic grotesque There was a vast amoung of dark wood siding, carved and fretted into crenelations, fenestrations, doodads, and whatnots There were probably a quaint old man and his quaint old wife hired by the week to dress up in peasant costumes made of litmus paper and pop in and out of opposite doors when the weather was about to change.

There were far too many shrubs on the lawn, clipped into cones, spheres, obelisks, cubes, and dodecahedrons; many of them wearing burlap burnooses to protect them from winter's freeze and windburn. In summer, no doubt, these would provide interesting backgrounds for hollyhocks, four o'clocks, and the other sorts of flowers that show up on greeting cards, in front of thatched cottages, with kitties and puppies and blue-eyed babes cavorting among them.

To complete the effect, a gaggle of gamins in long-tailed wool caps with bobbles on the ends ought to have rushed up carolling that here they came a-wassailing among the leaves so amply burlapped; but no gamins appeared. Nobody came at all, for quite a while. Max was wondering if perhaps he ought to direct his researches elsewhere when, sure enough, a rosy-cheeked moppet wearing a red velvet dress and pixyish red-and-white striped stockings came to open the door.

'Mewwy Chwiththmath,' she lisped.

'Mewwy Chriththmath to you,' Max replied. 'Is your gwandpa at home? Or are you the butler?'

'Who is it, Imogene?'

A stoutish young woman also wearing a regrettably snug-waisted red velvet frock and a pair of red-and-white striped stockings that made her legs look like a pair of warped barber poles came after the tot. Seeing Max, she snatched Imogene into the protection of her skirt.

'If you're from the press—'

'I'm Jeremy Kelling's nephew '

The little darling fought herself free of her mother's skirt and shrilled, 'He ith not! Thath the man who mawwied Couthin Tharah for her money.'

'Hush, Imogene,' chided the mother. 'We don't mention money in front of strangers. Anyway, you know perfectly well Cousin Sarah doesn't have any.'

'Then what did he mawwy her for?'

'Dearest, I don't know '

'Doth he?'

'Yes, but I'm not going to tell you,' said Max

He gave up on the moppet and turned to the mother 'Look, I know Dork's out of the hospital and I want to see him If you don't let me in, I'll get Jem to plant a rumour that you're giving the kid a toy Donald Duck for Christmas '

'You wouldn't!' gasped the woman

'Mama, he thaid a bad word,' squeaked her daughter

'Yes, and I'll thay it again if you don't get this show on the road pretty damn fast,' snarled Max 'Furthermore, where do you get that Cousin Sarah stuff? You're only her Cousin Lionel's wife's sister '

He knew her now It was the stockings that had temporarily distracted him. Her resemblance to Aunt Appie Kelling's daughter-in-law Vare was enough to give Max what a Scottish museum curator of his acquaintance had once alluded to as a cauld grue. The curator had been talking about a pop-art painting of a soup can, but Vare's sister looked enough like one in that outfit to justify the analogy That meant the precocious pimple at her knee was a first cousin to Vare's home-grown goon squad: Jesse, Woodson, James, and little Frank Those five mothers' darlings could well have got together last night to wreck the train and bump off its passengers as a way of beguiling a dull evening.

The theory was tempting but most likely not viable  Max gave Imogene his dirtiest look and addressed the mother in a Mike Hammer tone 'Are you going to let me in, or do I start quacking?'

'Ruffian!'

However, she got out of the way, dragging Imogene with her, and he entered without undue violence. The interior of Dork's house was about what he'd expected  Except for a dearth of ticket windows, it suggested Penn Station in the good old days, though on a smaller scale

The walls were loaded with framed photographs, some in colour, some black-and-white, some inexpertly hand-tinted All showed railroad stations with gardens around them

The furniture was of the pseudo-Jacobean style, running to nailhead  and cut plush upholstery in deep reds and olivey greens  If it hadn't been for the presence of the younger Mrs Dork, as Max assumed she must be, and her dimpled darling, he might have rather enjoyed the agreeably fusty waiting-room atmosphere  As it was, he simply wanted to do what he'd come for and get out as fast as he could

'Come along, Imogene,' he snarled  'Take me to your grandfather  And no funny business '

Automatically, the child tripped over to slip a tiny hand into his  Then she grabbed it back as if he'd been a hot stove 'Do I have to, Mommy?'

'Take him to Grandpa, Imogene  Please '

Lorista, that was her name  Max remembered her all too well now from one of Aunt Appie's dreadful tea parties, to which Kellings flocked in droves for some reason he still couldn't understand  She'd been wearing a grass-green dirndl that day, he remembered, and heelless black slippers with a seemingly endless crisscross of lacing over her thick white stockings. Or perhaps those had been her thick white legs  He'd stuck it out until Lorista produced her dulcimer and began singing folk songs. Then he and Sarah had told Aunt Appie they had urgent business elsewhere.

They'd gone back to Jem's, he remembered, and Jem had sung folk songs, too: 'Lisa and her Londonderry Air' and 'Never Go Walking Out Without Your Hatpin' Then Egbert had trotted out a hot Welsh rabbit and some excellent chenin blanc and they'd all drunk a toast to the frog in Lorista's throat He smiled at the memory as he followed Imogene past another gross or so of railway stations.

'Where's your grandfather?'

She shied nervously at the sound of his voice. 'In the conthervatory You're not weally going to—do that, are you?'

'Not if you behave yourself. Your grandfather knows who I am, by the way, so you needn't bother trying to rat on me He and I met last night at the Tolbathys' '

'Are you a Wussian?'

'You bet I am Is this the place?'

'Yeth,' she whispered.

'Okay, don't blow it.'

Max pushed open a heavy door and found himself at the flower show. In proportion to the rather small rooms he'd been walking through, the conservatory was immense. As another agreeable contrast, it was also warm. If there'd been any sunshine today, the glass roof and windows would no doubt have provided solar heat Since there wasn't, heavy insulating batts had been set in place to cover the glass, and some kind of central heating turned on

This must be where the Dorks really lived Max saw comfortable garden furniture set out on a flagstoned terrace in front of what was most likely a toolshed The little wooden enclosure had been got up to look like, naturally, a railroad station. It had a sign across the front that said, 'Dork's Depot.' It had window boxes full now of holly and ivy, and a prissy little border abloom with some white flowers Max couldn't recall ever having seen before.

'Hellebore,' said a somewhat hollow-sounding voice from a wheelchair that was drawn up beside a small ornamental pool complete with plashing fountain, live waterlilies, and goldfish. 'Christmas rose, you know Most people can't get 'em to bloom till Easter,' the voice added smugly

'Very lovely,' said Max, as in fact they were 'How are you feeling, Dork?'

'Rocky. You're Jem Kelling's nephew, aren't you?'

Imogene started to contradict her grandfather, then shut her little pink mouth and went over to adopt a winsome pose among the Christmas roses.

'Nephew by marriage,' Max amended to spike her infant guns 'Jem sent me along to see how you're doing.'

'That was kind of him And of you, to come. How is the old scorpion? Raising hell all over Phillips House, no doubt '

'No doubt whatsoever, I'm afraid He was in fair condition and rotten temper when I saw him a while back. By the way, I hope that wheelchair doesn't mean—'

'Doesn't mean a thing,' said Dork. 'I'm all right. A bit weak and dizzy, of course, from the indignities visited upon me at that butcher shop they call a hospital. Some nurse rolled me out in a wheelchair when they released me, so Lorista—my daughter-in-law—got the clever idea of putting me into this one when she and Immy got me home.'

'When was that?'

'Around nine o'clock this morning '

'And you've been here in the conservatory ever since?'

'Yes, and damned glad to be here, I can tell you. But come and sit down '

Dork wheeled himself over to the terrace and motioned Max into one of the aluminum mesh chairs. 'This thing does come in handy, I must say. We bought it for my wife's father when he came to spend his last years with us, as we thought But he died within a month, so we never felt we'd got our money's worth out of it till we started using it around the conservatory. It's a convenient way to go along the benches and attend to the plants without having to be constantly stooping over. See?'

Dork began scooting along the edge of the terrace, tidying away some wilted leaves on the foliage that surrounded it That gave Max a chance to view the celebrated hangnail. It was rather a disappointment, he thought; merely a hangnail of the second or third magnitude. Not, as Dictionary Johnson might have said, a hangnail to *invite* a man to Perhaps nobody but Jem would have thought it worth noticing, yet much might hang on that hangnail Max caught himself staring at Dork's left forefinger with such intensity that its owner noticed and scowled at the hangnail himself

'The mark of honest toil,' Dork half-apologized

'And well earned, I'm sure,' Max replied courteously 'Jem tells me you're quite a gardener Things pretty brisk around the potting bench these days?'

'No, not really It's too late for some things, too early for others. We generally give ourselves a rest over the holidays.'

Max picked up on the *we*. 'How's Mrs Dork? I wasn't able to get any report on her at the hospital '

'Oh, were you there? Dorothy's beginning to rally, they tell me, though she was much sicker than I last night '

'It's curious that so many of the wives got sicker than their husbands,' Max observed 'Are women more susceptible to colchicine poisoning than men, I wonder? Or are they more susceptible to caviar?'

'The latter, I suspect. Women tend to go in more for fancy foods, don't you think? I'd as soon have a paper of fish and chips on a bench by the tracks, outside some quiet little country station with the bees buzzing among the scabiosa and the ranunculus, myself.'

Max was not about to let Dork go wandering off among the scabiosa, nor yet the ranunculus 'Then you didn't eat much of the caviar yourself?' he asked.

'I didn't get much of it to eat. That ass Obed Ogham kept waving the waitress away.'

'Couldn't you have waved her back?'

'Not without creating a scene  You don't know Obed very well, I gather '

'I didn't know any of you until last night,' Max reminded Dork  'Besides, I gather I'm a member of the opposition, as far as Ogham's concerned. But you were with him from the time the caviar was served until the train stopped?'

'Well no, not all the time  That is to say, I clustered around with the rest of the party while that gussied-up waiter went through his routine of fetching the caviar  Hester expects us to, you know  Or perhaps you hadn't known, but you must have caught on  It's always a big thing with her  Anyway, I was with my wife then  I got Dorothy a glass of champagne when he started pouring it out, then went over to the bartender to get myself a Scotch and soda. By then Dorothy was chatting with some of her women friends, so I sauntered over and got into a huddle with Ed Ashbroom and Bill Billingsgate '

'What about Durward? Wasn't he with you, too?'

'Quent? He may have been  I can't recall offhand '

'He claims he was '

'Then I suppose he was, or thought he was, which would amount to more or less the same thing with Quent.'

'But surely you'd have noticed if he'd taken some part in the conversation?'

'No doubt, but he wouldn't have, you see  We were talking about delphiniums, and Quent can't tell one flower from another. No, that's hardly a fair statement  He'd know a rose, I'm sure, or a lily of the valley because of their distinctive fragrance  And perhaps a violet—'

'He'd be content just to stand there and listen to the rest of you talk about something he didn't know anything about?'

'Oh yes, just so he could hear our voices, you know. Quent's a dear chap. Anyway, Obed barged along with one of his stories, and when Obed's in full spate nobody else can get a word in anyway.'

'Did Ogham talk about gardening, too?'

'Perish the thought. Obed doesn't garden, and professes scorn for those who do. Sports are his big thing. He was a substitute tackle on the Dartmouth varsity his senior year Before your time, I expect '

'A man's man, is he?'

'You might call him that. Jem calls him other things '

'What things, Gwampa?'

Imogene, weary of disporting herself among the hellebore where nobody was paying any attention to her, had come back to swing on the arm of the wheelchair

'What what?' Dork smiled down at the child a good deal more indulgently than Max would have done. 'Quit joggling the chair, Immy You'll make your old grandpa seasick. Why don't you run and ask Mommy if it's time for my medicine? Shall she get something for you, Max? Tea? Whisky?'

'No, thanks I ought to be getting along. I don't want to wear you out.'

Max also wanted to catch the latest news on his car radio and find out what was happening at the hospital Still he paused. 'One thing before I go Would you happen to grow any meadow saffron here?'

'Meadow saffron? Oh, colchicum. Autumn crocus No, we don't grow it. Can't say I care for colchicum, myself. Rather a namby-pamby plant, I've always thought Wouldn't make much of a show in a station garden. Well, Max, nice of you to have dropped in Come again when I'm feeling better Bring that old reprobate Jem Give him my best and tell him to behave himself He'll have to, eh, with a broken hip? That will be a dreadful blow to the old wolfhound Show Mr Bittersohn out, Immy '

Immy was glad to oblige When they got to the front door, she stuck out her tongue in fond farewell. Max growled, 'Watch it, Ducky,' and got into his car with an agreeable feeling of something attempted, something done; even though a night's repose was still some hours and many miles away.

He'd been afraid he'd be too late for the news broadcast. However, he still had to listen through several commercials for used cars, Oriental rug merchants, and cough syrups doctors recommended most before he found out there had been no more deaths and another batch of patients were being sent home. The announcer sounded somewhat peeved about it

She did come up with one interesting scrap of information, though The late Edith Ashbroom, it turned out, had suffered from gout and had, in fact, been taking a medication containing colchicine Since colchicine is excreted slowly and converts in the body to oxydicolchicine (the announcer had trouble with that one), which can cause cell destruction in large doses, it was theorized that the colchicine in the caviar had mingled with that tongue twister already in her system and accounted for her having died while other victims were recovering

Max wondered if some die-hard anti-Communist was having an ideological struggle over having to be grateful to that mythical Russian who'd allegedly poisoned the caviar and provided him, (or her, unlikely as it might seem) with a beautiful cover for a possibly otherwise rather obvious murder He also wondered how many people beside himself were wondering who knew Mrs Ashbroom took colchicine, and who might have decided to give her a little more and see what happened.

He'd had Ashbroom next on his agenda anyway. He might as well go ahead with the visit. All he had to do when he got there was refuse anything to eat or drink, and watch out for karate chops.

# CHAPTER 20

Max passed through the intersection, where the catering shop appeared to be doing a booming business, and on up the hill to the big house with all the windows. Its many blinds were drawn now, and a man was up on a ladder, taking down some holiday decorations. He gave Max a surly glance but didn't say anything. Max watched him climb down and move his ladder on to the next wreath, then went up to the door.

It had a knocker, an enormous, highly polished brass one in the form of an abundantly fleeced sheep. That would be on account of the wool that had founded the Ashbrooms' joint fortune, no doubt. Max thumped the sheep a few times but nobody came, so he tried the doorbell.

This, after a while, brought results. A middle-aged woman in baggy corduroys and a filthy blue sweatshirt with 'Scrumptious' printed across the bosom snatched open the door, leaned out, and yelled, 'Quit lollygaggin' and get them wreaths down,' to the man on the ladder That done, she deigned to ask Max, 'What do you want?'

'I want to see Mr Ashbroom,' he told her.

'You can't. He's asleep.'

'I have a personal message for him.'

'You don't say  A spiritualist told me the same thing once. It was supposed to be from my dear departed Uncle Elmer  I knew it was a fake because he didn't ask for a loan.'

The woman buttoned her lips together and stood glowering at Max until he began to wonder if he ought to touch her for a few dollars to prove his bona fides. Then it occurred to him to try giving her some, instead.

'Put it against Uncle Elmer's outstanding account,' he suggested, handing over a ten. 'Going to let me in?'

She gave the note a careful going-over before she folded it and slid it into her pants pocket. 'You from the papers?'

'No.'

'Teevee?'

'No.'

'Too bad. I wouldn't o' minded gettin' my pitcher on the news. Who are you, then?'

'Jeremy Kelling's nephew  By marriage.'

'Why the hell didn't you say so in the first place? Keepin' a person standin' here in the cold freezin' her butt off. Come in an' park it someplace. Egbert send you?'

'Egbert has his hands full right now,' Max hedged. 'Did you know his boss is in the hospital?'

'No, but I ain't surprised. I figured it'd catch up with him sooner or later. What was it, hobnail liver or a mean-tempered woman?'

'A broken hip  He fell downstairs '

'Whose stairs?'

'His own '

'Huh, that's one I never expected  Stay here an' don't pinch nothin'  I'll go see if His Majesty's awake yet.'

'How long has Mr Ashbroom been home?'

'Too damn long, in my opinion  Frank went an' got him when they called up from the hospital early this mornin', wouldn't you know? We was figurin' on a nice quiet day an' maybe a double funeral to look forward to. He was bitchin' when he come into the house, an' he's been bitchin' ever since.'

'I thought you said he's been asleep.'

'He can bitch in 'is sleep, same as when he's awake. He's got a natural gift for it.'

'How do you know? Have you been listening to him?'

'Me? I got better things to do. I ain't supposed to be answerin' the door, neither. I only done it out o' the goodness o' my heart.'

'It was kind of you to take the trouble.'

She agreed that it was and went off somewhere, leaving Max in sole possession of the huge drawing-room where she'd parked him. It was a disappointment after the impressive exterior. Perhaps because the marriage of its owners had been merely a business proposition, the place gave no impression of harmony or comfort. Even that woman servant, as Max assumed she must be, was an incongruity although an enjoyable one  Max hoped she'd come back as chatty as she went.

However, she didn't come back at all. A grand lady in black manifested herself instead.

'Will you follow me, please?' she murmured in a chilly monotone.

Max obeyed, not trying to ask questions to which he knew he'd get no answers. She led him up a depressing staircase hung with tapestries that only a moth could love, to a bedroom that would have made a great setting for a game of Dungeons and Dragons.

The lord of this house of misrule lay propped up on a great many pillows against a rosewood headboard eight feet high and covered with knobs. He'd been sipping something from a tall glass. It smelled like the eggnog Sarah had sent Jem. If the man could drink brandy after having had his stomach pumped out, he couldn't have got that serious a dose of poison, or else he had a remarkably tough gut.

'Come in,' said Ashbroom, handing the empty glass to the woman in black. 'That will be all, Sawyer. Unless you'd like something, Bittersohn?'

'No thanks, I wasn't intending to stay long. How are you feeling?'

'How would anyone in my position feel? The shock of losing one's wife—'

'Yes, I can imagine.'

If Ashbroom was in shock, Max Bittersohn was Elisabeth Vigée-Lebrun  He offered a few conventional words of condolence, wondering if congratulations wouldn't be more in order, then said, 'Jem asked me to stop by and extend his sympathy, since he can't come himself. He hopes you're feeling as well as can be expected under the circumstances '

'It was kind of Jem to think of me.'

It would also have been kind of Ashbroom to ask after Jem, but he was too full of his own woes. 'This is a dreadful situation, coming out of the hospital after having escaped a horrible death by who knows how narrow a margin; only to be faced with having to bury your wife and file suit against your oldest and dearest friend.'

'You're suing Tom Tolbathy?'

'Of course Isn't everyone? I must say I believe I have the strongest case so far, however. You wouldn't happen to know whether any of the other victims has lost a spouse within the past couple of hours? I didn't catch the two o'clock news '

'You were too prostrated with grief to listen, I assume '

'Oh yes, totally prostrated.'

'How long does your lawyer advise you to remain prostrated?'

'He thinks I should make a brave effort to attend my wife's funeral Wednesday at ten o'clock, Saint Beowulf's I trust Jem understands it's his duty to be there, too. He'll have to hire an ambulance to bring him out here, I suppose. That should cost him a pretty penny Perhaps you'd be good enough to remind him his expenses won't be chargeable to the Comrades' treasury.'

'Won't they? Who's your treasurer?'

'I am. You might also remind him that he's required to wear the Great Chain.'

'I thought the regalia wasn't displayed in public.'

'The funeral will not be public I'm entitled to get my share of use out of the Great Chain, and I must insist on that right. I owe it to the memory of my departed spouse,' Ashbroom added with a brave effort to choke back his emotion.

'But what if the Great Chain hasn't shown up by then?'

'Then Jeremy Kelling forfeits his office as Exalted Chowderhead and a special election is called Jem will take it hard, I expect I feel for him, but we have to abide by the rules The Great Chain is Jem's personal responsibility during his entire term of office, as he was well aware when he accepted the honour.'

'The fact that somebody swiped the chain off him at the meeting doesn't constitute a mitigating circumstance?'

'Why should it?' Ashbroom asked in some surprise 'Good of you to have stopped in, Bittersohn. Give my regards to Sarah Please don't feel obliged to attend the funeral '

'Thank you for the dispensation,' Max replied humbly 'What about Miss Moriston?'

'What?'

'Miss Moriston. Your friend in Joy Street She asked me to let you know she's terribly worried about you Shall I tell her you're worried about her, too?'

'I was not aware of your acquaintance with Miss Moriston,' said Ashbroom 'I must say it comes as a surprise to me No doubt Sarah will be surprised, too, should I have occasion to mention it to her '

'Nice try, Ashbroom You know, I'm having a real problem here. Are you a first-class bastard or only a third-class bastard?'

'I shall see to it that you have every opportunity to clarify that point through due process of law if I find out you've been making any injudicious remarks concerning myself and Miss Moriston. Can you find your way out, or shall I call my chauffeur to assist you?'

'Please don't put yourself to the trouble I'll go quietly '

'Good. No hard feelings, you understand As a rule, I'm the most amiable of men, but one does have to protect one's interests. You won't forget to remind Jem about the Great Chain?'

'I never forget anything, Mr Ashbroom.'

He wouldn't forget this visit in a hurry, at any rate. Even if it had been one of the curmudgeonly leg-pulls the Comrades appeared to go in for, this was an inhuman sort of way to be joking, at a time like this. More likely, Ashbroom had deliberately gone on the defensive to keep Max from steering the conversation his own way. Miss Moriston had been only a useful diversion. What the hell, if he'd been waltzing her around to the Ritz in front of his buddies, he couldn't be much concerned about keeping his affair a secret. What Ashbroom had done was throw Max off the track, not so violently as when he'd got pushed into the Salvation Army kettle but just as effectively as he'd been led down the hill to Gerald Whet's.

But why? Had that really been Ashbroom in Boston, when he'd allegedly been here in Bexhill on his bed of pain? It wasn't impossible, especially if the chauffeur and that superior lady who was probably the housekeeper and possibly something else were cooperative A man who'd just taken sole charge of the family woolsack would have plenty to cooperate with, no doubt

There was no sense in Max's hanging around here trying to find out. It wasn't inconceivable that Ashbroom would call the police and have him pinched for loitering with intent That wouldn't go down well with the Comrades. Even if Ashbroom actually did intend to sue Tom Tolbathy, his clubmates would be apt as not to back him against an outsider The old tribal instinct was still mighty strong. Look at the way Jem and Obed Ogham stayed with the group even though they loathed each other's guts. What Max needed here was an undercover agent He wondered if Angie was still at the catering shop.

She was, he found out a couple of minutes later, and delighted to see him again even though she was frantically busy putting buttons on gingerbread boys.

'I just want to use your phone a second,' he explained, 'if you don't mind.'

'Be my guest.'

She waved him to a wall phone. Max tried Jem's home number and caught Egbert in the midst of mixing a batch of martinis

'I was just going to take them down to the hospital, Mr Max.'

'Let Jem wait a while and work up a thirst. This is more important. I've been talking to a lady friend of yours '

'Which one? I'm sorry, Mr Max, that sort of slipped out. Not that I'm any Don Juan, you understand; but being around Mr Jem all these years, it rubs off '

'I can see why it might. Anyway, this woman works for the Ashbrooms out here in Bexhill. She answered the door when I rang, but told me it wasn't usually her job to do so. She's about fifty-five, I'd say, not bad-looking but a casual dresser, has a lively tongue, and doesn't care much for her boss '

'That sounds like Guinevere '

'She looked more like Tugboat Annie '

'Oh yes, that would be Guinevere ' Egbert described the woman, down to the hairs in her nostrils 'Is she the one?'

'To a hair. What does she do around there?'

'Guinevere's the gardener. One of them, anyway. She must have been around to tend the plants in the greenhouse '

'Damn, I wish I'd known that when I was talking to her Look, Egbert, there are a few things I'd have liked to ask her, but I got thrown out before I had a chance Could you get hold of her?'

'I often have, Mr Max,' Egbert replied demurely.

'I meant by telephone I know it's less fun, but it's a hell of a lot quicker.'

'Yes, I can manage that '

'Good, then here's what I want to know.'

Max recited his litany, threw in a special reminder about the colchicum or autumn crocus, left money on the counter to pay for his call, told Angie to her expressed regret that he wouldn't bother her again, and left.

Obed Ogham was another important name on his agenda. After the going-over he'd got from Ashbroom, though, Max didn't think he'd fare any better with Ogham. He'd have to rely on another deputy. At the moment, he could think of only one who might conceivably be willing to take on the job Maybe it would be a mistake to trust Gerald Whet, but what else could he do? He turned the car around and went back past Ashbroom's house to the hospital

Security was less tight now Max had little difficulty wangling his way past the entrance He found Whet still at his wife's bedside and Marcia now able to manage a smile and a word of greeting. They chatted a moment, then he told Whet, 'Tom Tolbathy is tickled pink to have you stay. He suggests you borrow the Volvo to get back and forth in Why don't I drive you back there now to pick it up?'

'That's an excellent idea,' said Whet. 'Think you could get along without me for half an hour or so, Marcia?'

'Just barely '

There was a flash of the flirt in Marcia's reply Whet smiled for perhaps the first time since he'd left Nairobi, and went out with Max

Once they were outside, Max asked him, 'How'd you like to do me a favour?'

'Gladly, if I can '

'I want some information from Obed Ogham. There's no sense in my trying to approach him, but I expect he'd talk to you readily enough '

'What is it you want to know?'

Max explained. Whet nodded.

'I don't see any harm in asking '

'Good, then I'll phone you at the Tolbathys' later on. How soon do you think you might be able to get to Ogham?'

'That's a little hard to say, but I shouldn't think I ought to leave it too late. Everybody will be wanting to turn in early tonight. Myself included, if you want the truth. I'm still fighting my jet lag, and today's been a strain '

'I can well imagine,' said Max. 'You won't have any trouble getting to see him?'

'Oh no, I shouldn't think so. Obed and I aren't actually feuding, and my being at Tom's gives me a legitimate excuse to drop in on him. I can say Hester sent me to see how he's feeling. Then, since I wasn't at the party, it will be natural enough for me to get him talking about what happened. Persuading Obed to talk is never a problem,' he added drily. 'I'll just stay with Marcia till they come to fix her up for the night, then drop in at Obed's on my way to Tom's I can call you from Tom's, if you like.'

'Yes, why don't you?' said Max He wrote down his and Sarah's old number at the boarding-house and their new one at the apartment 'I should be at one of these. If by any chance I'm not, leave a message with Sarah.'


## CHAPTER 21

By now, Max could have driven that road to the Tolbathys' with his eyes shut, and was beginning to think he'd rather He dropped Whet at the house without going in himself and forged on to virgin territory The Billingsgates kept their bees and brewed their mead out in real farming country, twelve miles west of Bexhill. He wished they didn't. It was getting dark now, and the sky had a sullen look, as if it meant to start trouble and didn't care who knew it.

By the time he'd got to the Billingsgates', in fact, a few big flakes were splatting against the windshield. Great. Sarah would be worrying if he got caught out here in a snowstorm Actually, Max rather liked to think of her fretting about him, after all these years of batting around by himself. His mother had given that up when he was ten

Mrs Billingsgate—Abigail, as she insisted he call her—greeted Max at the door and acted well-nigh overjoyed to see him. He found this a welcome change, too, after the raking and harrowing he'd got from Edward Ashbroom. Abigail had been so sorry they hadn't had more chance to chat last night. She was happy to see him up and about. She herself, notwithstanding the stomach pump, was feeling chipper as one of her bees.

'Bounced right back as soon as I got home and ate some honey,' she told him. 'Honey's marvellous stuff. Never see a bee with a bellyache, do you? I've been dosing Bill with it, too.'

'How's Bill doing?' Max asked her

'Quite well He's out in the chapel just now, wrestling in prayer. I don't expect he'll be long He never wrestles very hard in this kind of weather Why don't I go and call him? We'll have tea with scones and honey by the fire in the keep.'

'The keep?'

'Yes, the castle's last refuge, you know. It's the only room we can sit in without freezing to death on a day like this. Come along and let me get you settled Unless you'd like to go along to the chapel and pray awhile first?'

'Thanks, but I'll settle for the tea I'm too tired to wrestle '

'But you haven't been sick like the rest of us, surely? I noticed you didn't eat any caviar '

'You did?'

'Yes, I'm very observant about what people eat. And drink Perhaps you'd dare to taste my homemade mead before you have your tea? Just a sip to warm you up.'

Before Max could refuse, she'd sat him down in a chair that would have made a reasonably impressive throne for an Anglo-Saxon king, and buzzed over to a cellaret that would have brought tears to the eyes of a Sotheby's auctioneer. She returned with two miniscule glasses, both of them brimming

'We really ought to have drinking horns, but when one's just back from having one's tummy vacuumed, one doesn't want to rely too heavily on the honey. Skoal.'

'If you say so ' Max took the thimbleful she handed him,

wondered briefly whether it was poisoned, then decided what the hell and took a sip. 'Very nice,' he gasped. The honey it was made from had, he presumed, been gathered by Italian killer bees.

As he was waiting for his eyeballs to settle back into their sockets, Bill Billingsgate appeared. In his wake came an esne—Max was sure the Billingsgates would employ nobody so modern as a housemaid—with a massive tea tray

'Ah, the guests are met, the feast is set ' Billingsgate came over to rub his hands by the fire 'Glad to see you looking so fit, er—'

'Jem Kelling's nephew Max,' his wife reminded him.

'To be sure Max My mind was temporarily abstracted. I've been wrestling in prayer.'

'So Abigail was telling me.' Max wondered whether he was supposed to ask who'd won, but decided he's better not 'You're looking well for a sick man, Bill. When did you get home?'

'We were fortunate enough to be among the first lot they let go Our daughter picked us up and had us home here by half past nine or so.'

'You've been in the house ever since?'

'Yes, and grateful to be here, I can tell you. Melisande stayed with us until after lunch. Then she decided Abby and I were both going to live and went off to deliver a few cases of mead to a Renaissance banquet in Worcester.'

'Is she coming back tonight?'

'No, Melly has a home of her own,' Abigail put in. 'And a family, too. They live in Shrewsbury. They'll be here for the holidays, though. I do hope you threw in a few words of thanks for our speedy recovery, Bill.'

'You may be sure I did, Abby.'

'I understand it's partly because you got stinted on the caviar, Bill,' said Max.

'We don't either one of us care much for it anyway, if you want the truth.'

'That's right,' said Abigail. 'We go in for the simple things of life.' She picked up the enormous silver teapot. 'Cream and sugar, Max?'

'Just plain, thanks.'

She raised her eyebrows but poured him a cup without the trimmings. Then she loaded her husband's and her own with spoonfuls of honey and cream so thick she practically had to dig it out of the jug before she began swabbing butter and honey on the hot scones.

Max managed to collar one for himself with no butter and only a modest freight of honey The honey was superb, he had to admit. The scones weren't bad either, though not up to Sarah's. With the fire in front of him, the mead inside him, and the snow beginning to fall in earnest outside the uncurtained windows, he was feeling like a character in one of the Christmas cards Sarah had been sticking up around the apartment every time she opened the mail One of them had a picture of the late Golda Meir on it His mother was not taking his marriage lying down

Those fields now getting a fresh coat of white would no doubt be abloom with some damn thing or other during the honey-gathering season. 'What sort of flowers do bees like?' he asked Abigail 'Do you grow colchicums, by any chance?'

'Autumn crocus?' She laughed. 'Heavens, no. I'm one myself and I don't care to be reminded. We grow mostly clover and the bees haven't complained yet. Here, take some more honey. That's not even enough to taste.'

Max thanked her for the honey and licked the edge of his scone so it wouldn't drip all over his pants. Then he remarked to his host, 'Your friend Dork says you were talking with him and Ogham and a couple of others when the train stopped, and that Ogham kept shooing the waitress away when she tried to pass you the caviar. Does that mean he doesn't care for it either?'

'It probably meant he'd had all he wanted for the moment and didn't want anybody else to get any in case he changed his mind later,' said Abigail, lathering herself another scone

'My dear, let's not fall into the sin of judging, especially since our new friend Max has set us so beautiful an example of Christian well-doing  I was sick, and ye visited me  Matthew 25:36.'

Max let that one pass  'I promised Jem I'd bring back a full report. He's frustrated, naturally, at not being able to check on his friends in person  So if you want to perform a real *mitzvah*, why don't you tell me everything that happened last night, from where you saw it  Can I assume Dork's information was substantially correct?'

'Precisely what did Dork tell you?' said Billingsgate with about the usual amount of genuine Yankee trustfulness

'The gist of it was that he, you, Ogham, Durward, and Ashbroom were standing off in a corner by yourselves talking about delphiniums for some while after the caviar had been served and until the crash took place. Except that he himself went and got drinks for himself and his wife, I think '

'That's not quite how it was. We all did a certain amount of shifting about, as I recall, though we gravitated back to our own little group  Dork did go up to the bar, I remember  He doesn't care for champagne, strange as it may seem. And Obed went and got drinks at least once. I recall his coming back with a glass in each hand, being, as he whimsically put it, a two-fisted drinker '

'And stuffed himself with caviar while he was near the source, I'll wager,' said Abigail  'That's why he refused any when it was passed.'

'Did you see him eating caviar?' Max asked her.

'Not I. I like to see people enjoying their food, as I told you, but it's no treat to watch Obed Ogham poke other people's bounty into that fat face of his as if he were stoking a boiler. And you needn't take at me about Christian charity, Bill, because you had plenty to say yourself that night we had the Comrades out here for the Renaissance Revel.'

'My dear, I don't profess to be a saint. And I must say

Obed would try the patience of Job himself when he starts being the life of the party. I see I shall have to go back to the chapel and sort out my feelings about Obed.'

'Have another scone first,' said his wife.

'Thank you, Abby,' said the good man, making no effort to stir from his easy chair, pricks of conscience notwithstanding. 'A good wife is above rubies. Thank goodness I've never had cause to rue by own wife's bees That's a little family pun, Max You'll forgive me, I hope. Now getting back to last night As I said, or did I? At any rate, it's my impression that each of the others left the group at one time or another I myself stayed put I'd found a cosy niche by the door where I could balance myself easily and enjoy the gentle movement of the train I had a glass of Tom's excellent champagne, which I prefer to sip slowly, being no great winebibber as Abby can tell you. I had no special hankering for any more caviar.'

'You had eaten some, then?'

'Of course, or I shouldn't have been sick I took one or two when the tray was first passed '

'That was before Ogham joined you?'

'It must have been, I should think, otherwise I mightn't have got any at all Good heavens, Abby, one might almost say Obed was being used as an instrument to protect his Comrades from the poison that might otherwise have slain us as it did Edith Ashbroom That is a solemn thought.'

'It sure bears thinking about,' said Max

If Ogham was being an instrument, why had he blown his horn among so small an audience? Of course he wouldn't have been interested in protecting Tom Tolbathy if he wanted control of Hester's money, but one might have thought he'd try to shield Hester herself from being poisoned. Unless she'd already made a will in his favour, and he knew it.

Abigail Billingsgate must have been thinking along the same lines as Max. 'I must say it strains my credulity to picture Obed Ogham as an errand boy for any ministering angel. Max, you're not eating a thing. Pass your cup, and let me fix you another scone. I can imagine what your uncle Jem would say to the notion of Obed's doing a gratuitous act of kindness, even under supernatural circumstances. All right, Bill, you can use me as a horrid example in your next sermon on malice toward none. Here, have some more honey.'

'Speaking of malice toward none,' said Max, 'you might try to convince your friend Durward he wasn't being deliberately slighted by the waitress  I understand he's none too happy about not being given enough caviar, even if it was poisoned.'

'That sounds like Quent,' Billingsgate admitted, taking more honey as bidden. 'Anybody but him would simply have gone and got some, or at least asked for it. Quent has this trying little habit of suffering in silence and not letting one know until it's too late to mend matters  We must make a special effort to have him out here during the holidays, Abby '

'I don't see why I should do penance for Quent's hurt feelings, Bill  You know perfectly well he'll bring his tree toad tapes  If we weasel out of listening, his feelings will be hurt again, and we'll be right back where we started '

'My dear, it's Christmas.'

'Bah, humbug! Don't try that Bob Cratchit routine on me. All right, my dear, since you insist on spreading sweetness and light, I'll invite Mabel Kelling here along with Quent.'

'Abigail, you wouldn't!'

'Why not? If you're determined on martyrdom, we may as well go the whole hog. Why can't we be charitable to Max and Sarah instead? You know, I don't believe I've seen Sarah since her mother's funeral  Such a quiet child, with those incredible hazel eyes and the most interested way of looking straight at you, as if she were wondering what kind of mythical monster you might be. I remember thinking she'd grow up to be a beauty Did she, Max? Mabel says not, but one can't go by what Mabel says.'

'I'll bring Sarah out and let you judge for yourselves. Now I'd better get going. She must be wondering what's keeping me. Thank you for the marvellous tea.'

'Thank you for coming to see us on such a wretched day. I hope you won't have any trouble getting back, in this snow. It's really coming down now, isn't it? Give Jem our very best. Tell him Bill will be in to see him as soon as he's fit to travel, and I'll go along to make sure Jem doesn't get subjected to pious utterances.'

'Abby!'

'Fiddlesticks, Bill. You know perfectly well Jem would benefit far more from a bottle of mead and a jar of honey than an earnest inquiry after the state of his soul. Come along, Max. If you must go, I'll show you out.'

'Please don't. I can find my way That fire's too comfortable to leave. Oh, Bill, just one question before I go. You haven't mentioned Edward Ashbroom. He was with you and Dork and the rest, he claims.'

'Ed?' Billingsgate splashed tea into his saucer. 'Why, I—I believe he did stop and chat for a while. Yes, of course. He must have If he says—'

Billingsgate's voice trailed off into silence Automatically the hand that wasn't holding the cup reached out for the honey jar Max decided it was in fact time to go, and went.

# CHAPTER 22

By the time Max had battled his way back to Boston and stowed his snow-caked car in its expensive niche at the parking garage, he was longing passionately for his own fireside. However, he decided he might as well complete the set before he signed off for the night. Quent Durward's feelings would no doubt get another bump if he found out he hadn't been grilled along with the rest of the boys.

Besides, Durward lived just beyond the hospital, over in one of the expensive apartments along the river. That meant a short but altogether too brisk walk with the wind whipping wet snow down the back of Max's neck despite Aunt Emma's woolly muffler. Max cheered himself with the thought that it would be worse going home with the snow in his face, and trudged on.

He'd had clients in this area, and managed to find Durward's address without much trouble Durward didn't have one of the penthouses, but he did have a corner apartment on a high floor with, no doubt, a magnificent view Max wondered whom Durward had got to decorate the place as a genuine E. Phillips Oppenheim setting for the sophisticated bachelor. There was even a houseman, maybe not Filipino but anyway Oriental, who seemed overjoyed at getting the chance to announce Jeremy Kelling's nephew.

Durward himself was delighted to have an unexpected guest. He appeared, after a short wait, in silk pyjamas, green morocco slippers, and a lounging robe the decorator must have picked out to go with the furnishings True to his role, he was cradling a stemmed cocktail glass in his left palm as he extended the right for a handshake.

'Come in, come in. This is neighbourly of you, I must say What will you have? I'm drinking soda water, myself, and trying to pretend it's champagne. A vain delusion, but I don't dare risk anything stronger after my night in the hospital How are you yourself feeling? I'm surprised to see you up and about in such weather.'

'Oh, I live just over the hill,' Max replied. 'No thanks, I won't have anything,' he told the hovering houseman. 'What time did they let you come home, Durward?'

'None too soon for comfort, I can tell you What a shame such a delightful evening had to end so wretchedly And the worst is yet to come, I suppose Three funerals, just at the height of the holiday season, and possibly more. One never knows with these insidious poisons. The after effects can be devastating, I believe. And all Tom Tolbathy's caviar being recalled from the shops. That's going to hurt him where he'll feel it most.'

'I think he's already too crushed at losing his brother to care much about the business,' said Max.

'But it was his great-grandfather's!' Durward sounded like an enraged chicken. 'My own great-grandfather's, too, if it comes to that. They started out as Durward and Tolbathy, you know.'

'Actually, I didn't.'

'Oh yes, we go all the way back to the early days of the China trade. Tea, spices, pepper, possibly a smidgin of opium but we don't talk about that.' Durward, the man of the world. 'Silks and chinaware and so forth, too, in the early days Like the Kellings, you know '

The you know's must have been rhetorical Clearly Durward didn't care whether Bittersohn knew or not; he was going to tell him anyway Perhaps with the Comrades he was content to hang around the fringes and listen, but now that he'd got an outsider's ear to bend, he made the most of his opportunity. While his host chattered on about fortunes won and lost, Max took visual inventory of his surroundings and decided the Durwards couldn't have been among the losers.

'Quite a place you've got here,' he observed when he saw a momentary opening between the junks and the sampans. 'All these big windows must be great for growing plants Are you a gardener like your friends.'

'Not I. They try to give me things, but nothing survives for long I've got so I simply tell them I can't be bothered. Anyway, *entre nous*, I can't see well enough to distinguish one from another. I like things I can touch and handle.'

That was obvious Durward could have started his own gift shop with the bibelots he had sitting around. Most of the figures showed monkeys and apes, some in grotesque positions, some dressed like humans, none of them the sort of thing Max himself would have cared to live with. A few were metal, but most were porcelain. It was perhaps a little surprising that a man who couldn't see well enough to water a plant chose to surround himself with so many small, fragile objects.

Durward was showing symptoms of wanting to discuss the collection in detail. Max decided this was getting to be over and beyond the call of duty.

'I really must be going. Glad to see you on your feet, Durward. Would you mind if I use your bathroom before I leave?'

'By no means. Oko, show Mr Bittersohn where to go '

'I can find it. Just point me in the right direction,' Max said.

Oko only bowed, grinned, insisted on accompanying Max to the useful door and pointing out the guest towels.

Max washed his hands, on which annoying traces of the Billingsgate honey had lingered, and dried them on one of the guest towels because he didn't want Oko to think he was a clod. While so doing, he took interested note of the accoutrements, which included a number of men's expensive toiletries, an electric hair-styling comb, an electric toothbrush, and another electrical gadget that first puzzled Max, then caused him to lift his eyebrows as high as they would go. So this was how Durward amused himself. No wonder he kept monkeys around. At last Max tried on a pair of glasses that had been left sitting on the sink, to see what looking at the world through the bottoms of two tonic bottles felt like, then went to put on the coat Oko was holding for him.

'Good night, Durward. I'm glad I'll be able to give Jem a good report of you.'

'Tell him I'm reasonably well, though somewhat frayed around the edges. Are you sure I can't persuade you to stop on for a bite of supper? Oko does a creditable egg foo yong, and I could play you some of my tree toad tapes.'

'Sounds great, but my wife is expecting me to take her out to dinner.'

'You're not going far, I hope, on a night like this.'

'No, just next door. Speaking of driving, did you have any trouble getting home, or were you back before it began to snow?'

'Missed it by hours. A friend drove me back quite early this morning One of our fellow sufferers, as a matter of fact He's a neighbour of the Tolbathys and lives just down the street from the Bexhill Hospital. We shared a room and they released the pair of us at the same time, so he called his house and had his chauffeur bring the car around.'

'He came with you?'

'Yes, I was very much surprised I assumed he'd have the chauffeur drop him off first, but he said he had urgent business in town, though naturally I didn't ask him what it was. Anyway, he was going to take care of it, then go home and rest. Remarkable stamina, I must say By the time I got home, I couldn't have licked a postage stamp.'

'Was this Ed Ashbroom?' Max asked.

'That's right. You must have met him last night. Oh, and by a curious coincidence, we passed Gerry Whet on the street, though I don't believe he saw us That's Marcia's husband, you know. I didn't actually notice him myself, but Ed remarked on it. We'd both thought he was still in Nairobi. Small world, as they say.'

'Very,' said Max. He took his hat and gloves from the affable Oko, thanked Durward for his invitation to drop in again soon and hear the tree toads, promised to give Jem all sorts of wishes for a speedy recovery, and at last managed to pry himself loose.

The walk back was every bit as bad as Max had expected it would be. By the time he got back to Tulip Street, he was covered with snow and Sarah was having fits.

'I thought you were freezing to death out in the wilds of Bexhill. Here, give me that coat. I'll hang it over the bathtub so it won't drip all over the floor. Brooks is hanging the last curtain and we're going to have a drink. Want one?'

'Drink to me only with thine eyes '

Max pulled his wife tight against him and beguiled a satisfactory few minutes forgetting the cares of the day. 'Okay,' he said at last, 'what are we waiting for? Where's the hooch?'

'In the bottle,' Sarah told him 'Pour one for yourself and Brooks, and a sherry for me I have a few things to do in the kitchen.'

'Aren't we eating with the gang?'

'No, do you mind? Two of Mrs Gate's nieces popped in from Delaware for a surprise visit. She wanted to invite them to dinner at the house since she's really too frail to go out in this weather, and you know that dining-room doesn't seat more than ten comfortably. I told Theonia we'd come another night.'

'Fine with me. I'm sure we can find some way to entertain ourselves '

Pleased by this agreeable turn of events, Max went to get the drinks and greet his particular favourite among the cousins-in-law. 'What ho, Brooks  Thanks for doing my chores for me. How about a restorative?'

'Splendid suggestion.'

Brooks was a chipmunk of a man, spruce and sleek and quick for his age  He took the drink, gave Max a brisk nod, and sat down in one of the chairs Sarah had arranged around the gas log that had mercifully escaped being renovated out of existence any time during the last seventy or eighty years.

They liked the gas log. Sarah, after years of cleaning out fireplaces both at the old Tulip Street house and the place at Ireson's Landing, was as well pleased not to have the bother of firewood and ashes. Max, the least domestic of men, found those neat little rows of blue-flame teeth quite cosy enough for practical purposes. Furthermore, gas didn't pollute the air quite so much as unburned wood particles, as Brooks pointed out They toasted their feet, sipped at their drinks, ate the cheese and crackers Sarah put out, and were happy

'Anybody go over to see Jem this afternoon?' Max asked after a while

'Theonia was there about three o'clock,' Brooks told him 'The therapist had Jem up in the walker She said it was heart-wrenching.'

'Was Jem in terrible pain?'

'No, he was in excellent voice '

'Oh Tough Did Theonia find out when they're going to let him out?'

'As soon as possible is what the doctor said, and I'm sure he meant it. I only hope Jem's not going to be subjected to any further shenanigans when he gets there. Max, what do you think of that colchicine business? You're not swallowing that Russian plot to destroy the capitalist caviar consumers?'

'Would you? I'm not sure I swallow the gout medicine, either. I've been nosing around among Jem's gardener friends all afternoon to see if I can find one who grows colchicums None of them has admitted it, naturally '

Brooks emitted a gentlemanly snort. 'Bless you, my boy, anybody on earth can grow a colchicum. In fact, given a bulb, there's no way you can't.'

'What do you mean?'

'The colchicum, unlike the crocus which it resembles but isn't related to, has the peculiar habit of growing when it gets ready to grow, regardless of whether you bother to plant it or not. You know how an onion, for instance, will sprout if you keep it around the kitchen too long? Well, a colchicum bulb looks something like an onion, and it not only sprouts but it blooms. Basically, all you have to do is not throw it away.'

'Where do you get these bulbs?'

'Garden shops, places where they sell plants, maybe even in the five-and-ten. They're not hard to come by.'

'Are the flowers poisonous as well as the bulb and seeds?'

'Oh yes. According to my reference, all parts of the plant are toxic.'

'What would happen if you crumbled one up and mixed it in with the egg yolk?'

'You'd make people sick. Good thinking, Max And I suppose you could chop up the bulb and mix that with the onion. I have no idea what colchicum tastes like and no wish to find out One assumes the strong flavour of the caviar was sufficient to mask it You know, Max, I think that must have been how it was done Egg yolk and onion would be the perfect camouflage, just as that silver chain was an ideal disguise for the poisoner '

'What do you mean?' Sarah asked him.

'By showing up dressed as a wine steward, he must have looked impressive and somehow official. Without it, he might have come in for some embarrassing questions from the caterers. They might even have gone to ask Mrs Tolbathy if they had to take orders from him, and of course that would have ruined his plan even if it didn't get him into serious trouble As to poisoning the garnishes, that would be a snap once he'd got his hands on them I could do it like nothing at all '

'But you're a magician,' Sarah objected She meant that literally In his leaner days, Brooks had often eked out his income doing magic tricks at children's parties.

'This fellow was a magician, too Rather a good one, in my opinion By wearing that chain, he made a trainful of people see a wine steward who didn't exist. By taking it off, he made the wine steward disappear. By making a great show of proving the caviar itself couldn't have been tampered with after it left the cannery, he distracted attention from the garnishes. It's simply misdirection, you know He could have poisoned the dishes in full sight of the passengers, though I suspect he did it while he was carrying the tray from the caboose to the dining car. Did anyone go with him to hold the door, Max?'

'No. The women were busy and the tray wasn't large. There was also a lavatory he could have ducked into.'

'He wouldn't have had to,' said Brooks. 'It was a piece of cake. He'd have had the doings ready in little plastic bags, no doubt, palmed them before he picked up the tray, and dropped them into the dishes while his back was turned to the women in the caboose, just before he went into the dining room. As he set the dishes on the epergne, I expect he stuck in little silver serving spoons. That's when he'd have stirred the poison in A quick fluffing would do it.'

'If it didn't get thoroughly stirred, that would account for the fact that some passengers got sicker than others,' said Sarah, 'even if they ate the same amount of caviar '

'Oh yes, no question. Apparently he didn't care who got sick or died as long as somebody did, which is a charming thought. As for himself, he'd be counting on the fact that plant poisons usually take a while to start working That would mean the dishes would probably be cleared away, as in fact they were, before the effects began making themselves felt. Colchicine would normally take a fair while longer than it did in this case I believe, but the fact that people had had nothing else to eat and a fair amount to drink probably speeded up the process Not to mention the shock of that jolting stop, and no doubt the chain-reaction effect of seeing others get sick. It was a terrible thing to do, Max, but you must admit it was cleverly done. Is that your oven timer, Sarah, or the telephone?'

'It's the phone,' said Max. 'I'll get it. I'm expecting a couple of calls.'

'When were you ever not?' Sarah asked, giving him a pat in passing.

It was Gerald Whet reporting on Obed Ogham. Max listened, scowled, said, 'Thanks,' got a dial tone, and called Egbert.

'Hi, how did you make out? She did? You dog, you! About Ashbroom, did she—she's positive? I see. Where are you

now? Oh, Christ! No, it's okay. Stay where you are. I'll get
back to you later.'

He put down the receiver and headed for the bathroom to
get his wet overcoat.

'Sorry to run out on your dinner, kid, but I think I'll take a
run down and see Jem before the storm gets any worse  He
sent Egbert home as soon as it began to snow.'

'But Max,' Sarah protested, 'it's absolutely beastly out
You can't even see the sidewalk, I just looked. It won't kill
Uncle Jem to stay alone for one evening.'

'Want to bet? Stay with her, will you, Brooks?'

'No he won't,' said Sarah. 'If you must go, I'm going with
you '

'So am I,' said Brooks  'I'll just step next door to get my
galoshes and make my apologies. Meet you downstairs in
precisely forty-five seconds '


## CHAPTER 23

Max wasted no time trying to argue them out of going. He
just crammed Sarah into her coat and boots and hustled her
downstairs. They collected Brooks two seconds before the
appointed time and set a pace as fast as the horrendous
walking would allow: Max keeping a tight hold on Sarah and
lifting her over the drifts when she floundered, Brooks pretending he was stalking a snowy owl in flight

Though the distance wasn't much, they were all worn out
when they got to the hospital  They wasted no breath on
talking but pounded the snow off each other's clothes and
grabbed the first elevator they could get

'Max, what's the matter?' Sarah managed to gasp as they
were getting off at Jem's floor.

'I've set your uncle up for the murderer, that's all  Look,
there he is!'

Sarah emitted a half-hysterical giggle. A figure wearing a long coat, a vast red-and-white striped muffler with the ends trailing halfway to his knees, and a Lincolnesque stovepipe hat was emerging from the men's room and scuttling along the corridor ahead of them.

'But that's Scrooge. Oh, Max!'

'Sh-h.'

They must look like a chorus from *The Pirates of Penzance*, Sarah thought wildly as the three of them tiptoed after the bundled-up caricature. The evening meal was over by now, and visitors were being kept away by the storm. There was nobody else in sight at the moment except a ward maid stacking used supper trays on a trolley. Intent on her work, she didn't even glance up at the strange procession.

Scrooge didn't look around, either, but strode briskly, straight to Jeremy Kelling's room. As he turned in at the doorway, those behind him caught sight of a face too Scrooge-like to be real

Max beckoned his cohorts on at a rush, but held them outside the door. There at the foot of Jem's bed stood Scrooge. Jem, who must have been taking a postprandial snooze, opened his eyes, goggled up at the apparition, and beamed

'Bah, humbug, Comrade!'

The tall hat bobbed in acknowledgment of Jem's greeting, but Scrooge didn't speak. A gloved hand came out of the right overcoat pocket and tossed a brightly wrapped package on the bed. It fell with a heavy clank Jem reached out for the gift, but the glove was sternly pointed at a big label that read, 'Do Not Open Until Christmas.'

The other glove came out of the left-hand pocket, bringing forth two more presents. One was small and labelled, 'Eat me.' The other was gurgly and labelled—quite superfluously, it would seem, in Jem Kelling's case—'Drink me.' Scrooge laid these on the bed table, and, still without speaking, turned to go. That was when Max grabbed him. He was not easy to hold

'My God, he's strong! Brooks, get that scarf off and pin his arms. Watch out for a karate chop.'

'What the hell are you doing?' Jem was bellowing. 'Stop it, Max, that's one of the Comrades.'

'Which one?'

'How the hell do I know? Let him go He's only joking '

'I'm not Don't touch those packages.'

'But they're for me.'

'Damn right they are. I want them analysed. Quit kicking, damn you,' he barked at his captive. 'Brooks, take my belt and strap his legs together.'

Scrooge struggled ferociously but Max was powerful, Brooks was wily, and Sarah was inspired to bop the captive over the head with a jugful of ice water They got him down on the floor, crudely but thoroughly trussed, while Jem pounded on his call button with might and main

'My God, Max, do you mean this was another try at killing me?'

'Oh yes. Couldn't resist a shot at a sitting duck Could you, Durward?'

Max ripped off the latex mask that covered the attacker's head. Even then, Jem was unconvinced.

'What do you mean Durward? That can't be Quent. He's not wearing glasses. Quent can't see without them.'

'He couldn't see with them either, according to you and your Comrades In fact, he sees plenty now that he's got contact lenses. And a cute little dingus to wash them in, that he forgot about when he let me use his bathroom a while ago.'

By now two nurses, an intern, and the ward maid were crowding into the room. 'Call the police,' Max told them. 'This man was trying to kill my wife's uncle.'

'I'll get Security.' One of the nurses flew out to the desk.

'I'll get a mop.' The ward maid sensibly began coping with the slippery puddles of water and ice on the floor.

The intern obligingly sat down on Durward to hold him still until the security guard arrived a couple of minutes later.

'What's this about a murder?'

'This jokester here,' said Max, 'has already been responsible for Mr Kelling's broken hip. This time, he evidently meant to do a more thorough job. I want those packages analysed right away, and I want the prisoner held until we get a report.'

'What would you say is in the packages?'

'That largest one contains a silver chain stolen from Mr Kelling this past week. It's probably booby-trapped in one way or another, and should be handled very carefully. The other packages are obviously food and drink of some sort. Both should be tested first for colchicine, since he's already used that successfully. His name is Quent Durward, he lives just over the way,' Max gave the address, 'and he has a houseman I want picked up immediately as a material witness. The man is probably Durward's karate instructor, among other things. Got that?'

'I get it,' said the guard. 'Anything else?'

'Yes. After you get Durward stowed away, call up the Bexhill police chief and give him a nice, fat raspberry for me.'

'Bexhill? You mean the town where all those people on the train got poisoned by some crazy Russian?'

'It wasn't a Russian, it was this man right here. What was your motive, Durward? Or were you just doing it as a joke?'

At last Durward spoke up for himself. 'Look at that thing on the bed,' he shrieked. 'Calls himself a Scrooge. Bah, humbug! He couldn't be rotten if he tried. Can't hate, can't kill, doesn't even know enough to die. Damn you, Jem Kelling, why didn't you let me murder you? Disgusting little woman-chaser. And they elected you Exalted Chowderhead, so you could look down on me. Poor old Quent. Wouldn't let me be Marley's Ghost. Wouldn't listen to my tree toads. Mocked me because you thought I couldn't see. I've been laughing at you all for a long time now. And don't think this is my last laugh. I'll get you yet. I'll kill you all! Bah, humbug, you old fool. Bah, humbug.'

Even with the shot of tranquillizer the intern had to give him, Durward was still screaming, 'Bah, humbug!' when the police dragged him away in a straitjacket.

## CHAPTER 24

'I told you so, didn't I?'

Jeremy Kelling was cock of the walk, back in his own flat with his leg on a hassock and his hand on a glass Egbert had summoned a sizeable welcoming party: Max, of course, and Sarah looking lovely in a red Christmas frock, and Brooks with his hair slicked down, and Theonia unutterably gorgeous in a dinner gown she'd fashioned from two crepe de Chine chemises and a pair of green satin lounging pyjamas dating from the Ann Harding era, which had formed part of Sarah's Aunt Caroline's wedding trousseau.

Cousin Dolph and his wife Mary had stopped in but couldn't stay. They were giving a dinner at the Senior Citizen's Recycling Centre for some of Mary's former colleagues. Dolph was going to be Santa Claus. He'd auditioned his ho-ho-ho amid tumultuous applause and let Jem wear his whiskers for a while before they'd left.

Gerald Whet was there with Tom Tolbathy, both of them looking far fitter than they had a day or two ago Marcia was to be released from the Bexhill Hospital the next morning Hester was already at home, being pampered by her adoring daughters-in-law and the grandchild who'd so luckily escaped being poisoned on the train. Hester had sent Jem a vast hamper of imported goodies, but no caviar.

The recall had been quashed, of course, as soon as Quent Durward's dastardly deed had been made public, but Tom said Hester was going to wait a long time before she dragged out her great-aunt's epergne again.

'Quent's confessing all over the place,' Whet told the

party 'I made a detour over to the Charles Street Jail on my way here, and was told they're thinking of transferring him to Bridgewater State Hospital for the criminally insane. He's gone completely around the bend, it appears, and keeps insisting he only wanted to show the Comrades how Scrooge really ought to be played. He's claiming it was all our own fault for electing you instead of him as Exalted Chowderhead, Jem, and that he had to eliminate you for the good of the club He actually did mean for you to die, they say '

'I'd begun to suspect he might,' Jem replied soberly despite the five martinis he'd had so far.

There had, as expected, been colchicine in both the bottle of gin and the cheese spread Durward had brought to the hospital There'd also been something extremely nasty on the points of the tacks he'd inserted between the links of the Great Chain before he'd gift-wrapped it to take back to Jem Kelling.

His plan had been, no doubt, simply to deliver his packages and get out of the hospital, counting on the storm to keep visitors away from Jem. Knowing his Comrade, he'd been confident the Exalted Chowderhead would immediately rip open the gifts, put on the chain, and take a swig from the bottle.

Sooner or later, a nurse would come along and find she'd lost a patient. Nobody would know where Jem had got the lethal presents. If anybody had seen Durward in his Scrooge getup, they'd have thought he was just some entertainer trying to cheer up the patients. There were enough of such things going on at holiday time. As a last resort, Durward could have tried framing somebody else, just as he'd attempted to finger Ashbroom or, alternatively, Whet for the previous murders.

'Do you think that man is really insane, Max?' Sarah asked.

'His vanity must be pathological, anyway. You pointed

that out, Jem, when you told me how Durward refused to admit he was legally blind. That was true for several years, by the way. They've turned up his records at the Eye and Ear Infirmary. It's only within the past couple of years, with the new microsurgery and improved contact lenses, that his vision has been drastically improved.'

'Too bad he couldn't have put it to better purpose,' said Gerald Whet. 'And to think Quent went right on pretending he could hardly see his hand before his face. That's a bit crazy, surely?'

'I don't know,' said Max. 'It gave him a certain power he'd never had before, I suppose, being able to see when you all thought he couldn't He could get away with things that seemed impossible for him, like his impersonation of the wine steward on the train. And that chase he led me all over Beacon Hill on Sunday morning I don't know whether he was pretending to be you, Gerry, or Ed Ashbroom, though he did try to steer me on to Ashbroom later '

'How was that?'

'He told me a stupid lie about Ashbroom's having driven him to Boston, when he must have known the servants, notably Egbert's lady friend Guinevere, could swear their boss was back in Bexhill making himself obnoxious at the time. Incidentally, Egbert, that call to Guinevere helped save Jem's life So did the one you made about Obed Ogham, Gerry Once I knew those two were out of the running, I realized it had to be Durward That's when I panicked '

'Damn lucky for me you did,' Jem grunted. 'He had me fooled completely. And that's not easy, I can tell you.'

'I know,' said Max. 'You wouldn't have let him shove you into a Salvation Army kettle, as I did '

'A Salvation Army kettle?' Cousin Theonia raised her delicately pencilled eyebrows. 'What a remarkably inconsiderate thing to do. Unless of course he is totally deranged and cannot be held accountable,' she added, for Theonia believed in giving everyone the benefit of the doubt.

'I think he's going to have a hell of a time copping a plea,' said Max. 'Some interesting information's come up about a rival importing firm he's bought into. Whatever his other motivations, it appears Durward's primary one was to put the Tolbathys out of business.'

'But why?' said Tom Tolbathy 'Good God, the market would have been big enough for both of us. We're not aggressively competitive '

'From a conversation I had with him shortly before he made his call on Jem, I'd say Durward's been carrying a grudge all his life because his great-grandfather sold out too soon, and because the Tolbathys started doing a hell of a lot better once the Durwards weren't in the business to keep fouling things up. He saw your success as one more humiliation for himself.'

'But Tom and Wouter never humiliated him,' Gerald Whet protested. 'None of us did. When you've been schoolboys together, you feel privileged to tease each other a bit, but it's all in fun. Couldn't Quent realize that?'

'I've always thought an inability to laugh at yourself must be the greatest curse a human being can bear,' Brooks observed.

'And how right you are, my darling,' cooed Theonia, settling the lace at her throat with a graceful hand 'But you know, Max, I am still puzzled as to how Mr Durward managed all those dreadful deceptions. What intrigues me most is how he managed to steal that enormous chain right off our dear Jeremy's neck. It must have been a truly ingenious piece of legerdemain.'

'Leger de magnet, you might say,' Max told her 'I caught on to that trick when I was looking at Wouter Tolbathy's electric trains. He worked them on a system of micromagnetic solanoids, so that they could be connected and disconnected by remote control. Wouter was remarkably clever at that sort of thing, and I'm afraid that's what killed him.'

'But how?' asked Tom Tolbathy. 'Oh my God! You mean—'

'That's right. They had it apart down at the station Apparently when you were Exalted Chowderhead last term, Tom, Wouter managed to get hold of the Great Chain. That wouldn't have been hard, I don't suppose '

'Oh no,' said Tom. 'I'd never have locked anything away from Wouter.'

'Well, just for kicks, I suppose, Wouter took apart the Codfish pendant, which was moulded around a hollow centre as such things often are, and built a miniature transmitter into it. He then separated two of the links in the chain and reconnected them by means of tiny electromagnets.'

'That meant the chain could be opened and closed by a handheld remote control device,' Brooks explained to Theonia.

'How clever. But why?'

'Sometimes it was hard to know why Wouter did anything,' Tom admitted. 'Often, I think, it was just for the fun of the doing. But then he'd think of some way to put it to use ' The bereft brother smiled sadly 'Wouter could always think of something.'

'In this case, it appears to have been Durward who thought of something,' said Max. 'Maybe Wouter was careless about trying out the coupling in front of him or something, assuming Durward wouldn't see well enough to notice.'

'And not knowing Quent had a scheme of his own up his sleeve,' said Jem.

'Right. Anyway, Durward learned the Comrades now owned a trick chain and either egged Wouter on to make it disappear at your Scrooge Day luncheon or else got hold of the control gadget and worked the catch himself. It would have been easy enough for him to be standing next to Jem when the chain fell off, scoop it up, and stuff it inside his pantleg or somewhere.'

'I expect Wouter helped Quent steal the chain from me at the luncheon,' said Jem. 'He'd have thought Quent meant to make the chain reappear as soon as they figured out the most embarrassing way to do it.'

'You're probably right,' Max agreed. 'Only Durward had other plans That's why he decided he'd have to kill Wouter, though I still can't figure out why he felt it necessary to wear the Great Chain to poison the garnishes for the caviar. Sarah claims it's because he didn't want to spend the money on something he'd never wear again.'

'He may not have wished to risk being identified by a shopkeeper if he bought or rented one,' Brooks suggested.

'I wonder if it could have been some kind of revenge on the rest of us, for teasing him about his poor eyesight, which I'm afraid we did on occasion,' Tom Tolbathy said 'You know, flaunting the Great Chain in front of us and having nobody notice simply because he'd taken off the Codfish. That would have been one reason why he wouldn't dare let Jem come to the party Jem would surely have spotted it '

'Damn right,' said Jeremy Kelling. 'He'd never have worked his foul stunt if Old Eagle-Eye had been aboard. You noticed at the hospital, Max, that he was careful not to leave any part of himself visible The one thing that misled me was his not wearing glasses with that mask. I still can't believe he managed to find me without them.'

'That's because you never happened to look through the ones he's been wearing lately,' said Max. 'I had the chance when I dropped in on him unexpectedly He'd left a pair in the bathroom I took a look and realized they were only thick windowpane. I don't know why he kept on wearing them after he'd got his contacts. Either he felt naked without them, or else it amused him to let you go on thinking he was still visually handicapped when in fact he could see as well as the average person of his age.'

'Devious bastard,' snorted Jem 'Egbert, why the hell don't you open that hamper of Hester's and fix us something to eat? I'm hungry, damn it. Hey, this is the first time I've felt like eating since I broke my goddamn hip. I must be getting better. Whoop, whoop, halloo!'

'Halloo yourself, you damned old fool,' said Formerly Exalted Comrade Tolbathy, blowing his nose violently. 'Jem, we've got to talk about Wouter's funeral. You'll deliver the eulogy, of course, wearing the Great Chain. And I thought Gerry might pull the dragon in behind the coffin. As you finish talking, maybe you could flip the switch and let it breathe a little fire and smoke. I think Wouter would have liked that, don't you, fellows?'

'Hell, yes,' said Jem. 'Wouter would have done the same for us. Fill 'em up, Egbert. Let's have one for old Wouter.'

The Exalted Chowderhead raised his glass on high. 'Bah, humbug, one and all.'

And nobody could doubt that he meant it.

# COMING SEPTEMBER 2003

## *THE PLAIN OLD MAN*
by Charlotte MacLeod
ISBN: 0-7434-7479-1

### A SARAH KELLING AND
### MAX BITTERSOHN MYSTERY

Sarah's Aunt Emma's theater troupe is doing Gilbert and Sullivan's *The Sorcerer*, as Emma has always hankered to play Lady Sangazure. Perhaps she made a bad choice, though, by casting a well-connected con man in the title role. It's no mere evil spell that leaves Charlie Daventer dead on his bathroom floor. But the show must go on.

Cousin Frederick is hurled into the breach. Old Fred really can't tolerate the general assumption that his friend Charlie died by accident. He convinces Sarah that a murder has been committed. Sarah's husband, Max the detective, is off in Finland, so she tackles the case herself.

Clues aren't hard to find. Sarah sorts them out, only to learn when the curtain falls that the show is far from over. . . .